Main Suspect

May'lon "Maze" Miranda

authorHOUSE®

AuthorHouse™
1663 Liberty Drive
Bloomington, IN 47403
www.authorhouse.com
Phone: 1 (800) 839-8640

Published by AuthorHouse 08/27/2016

ISBN: 978-1-5246-2622-8 (sc)
ISBN: 978-1-5246-2621-1 (e)

Print information available on the last page.

This book is printed on acid-free paper.

This Book is Dedicated to the Loving Memory of

Louis and Anna Miranda

May you both Rest in Peace

See you both when I get there

This Book was inspired by my good friend

Neil Alexander

Thank you for the Inspiration

I took all the negative situations in my life on this planet and turned them into positive situations so that not only my children won't make those same mistakes as I did but in the process help others as well. To all my readers and supporters I say THANK YOU!!!!!!!!

– May'lon "Maze" Miranda

My name is Jacob G. Cass the III I am an attorney, a defense Attorney. In fact I am one of the best attorneys in Washington State. You know what who am I kidding? Outside of Johnny Cochran I'm the best hands down in the country I mean it. I've been with my law firm Almonds & Almonds for 11 long years as a defense attorney I have never lost a case straight out of Law School. I always questioned my boss as to why I never made partner? I guess being that I was the only black face at the firm they wanted to keep me as their work horse. But I knew my time would come because I brought in all the clients, all the best cases, so it was only a matter of time. But as good as I was as an attorney it's funny because this was never the dream I had in mind for myself. I actually was a hell of a ball player and wanted to play pro ball, yes that's right I wanted to be a Hoya. So you're probably wondering how do I go from wanting to be a professional basketball player to becoming a Lawyer? Well in order for me to explain that I'm going to have to take you back way back to about Middle School maybe even younger because I've really tried to block the thoughts and memories out of my mind so bare with me. Well I grew up in Aberdeen Washington it was me and my mother. As far as my father goes well let's just say he couldn't take it anymore as I saw it let me explain. I must of been about 13 at the time so this would make my friend at the time around 8 because we were five years apart. For the most part we were best friends he was my only friend we did everything together he was like a brother to me. Aberdeen is a very small city if you like the country you would love it there, if you like city life this would be hell for you. The city is so small it almost feels as if everybody here knows everybody here. My father Jacob Case the second worked in a steel mill he was a very hard worker with very little education but busted his ass to make a buck and to provide for our family as best as he could. He was very old fashioned and didn't want my mother to work at all. He believed that as the men we are the providers of our family that a woman should stay home keep up the home and raise the children that was just how he saw it. I remember as a child he would always tell me to never work in no steel mill, as I would always want to go with him to work and help out. He would tell me to never be like him to get an education and always strive to be better than he could ever be. So because of how hard he would push me I was always in the books and never had many friends and never did much. Anyways like I said before as a kid I loved basketball because my father did as well and put me onto it. He would always watch basketball games on television and id always watch it with him. My friend and I one day he surprised us and come home with a basketball hoop and my friend and I went ape shit over it we were so happy. But there was only 1 rule my father had about this hoop and that was that my friend and i were never allowed to play outside on it unless either he or my mother were present outside with us. So you could only imagine how hard that was on us as little kids. The reason for him not wanting us to play without supervision is because we lived by a major road that was very busy and it was very dangerous. Well one day after school one afternoon my friend and I wanted to play some ball. My father was away at the mill, and my mother was fast asleep. Now I never ever went against anything that my father ever said but this particular day I couldn't resist it and I saw an opportunity to play without supervision as I thought to myself I'm old enough to play on my own. So I remember grabbing the basketball then running outside and playing. It was so much fun and I felt like I was free and on top of the world. I said to myself I wish my dad would have more trust in me and allow me to be careful enough to the point where I could do this more often without me having to hide what I am doing. I felt guilty for lying to my father I didn't want to hurt or disrespect him but I loved basketball so much. My plan was to finish playing before he got home from work or my mother got up, I got my friend out and he and I played for hours. Now being so into what I was doing having all this free fun and the fact that my mother was sleeping I lost track of time and before you knew it here comes my father pulling up into the driveway. So my friend and I shocked scared to death both run for the house front door and jet to the room. I'm saying to myself "oh my god" dad saw me and is going to be so mad, So disappointed in me, plus I had my friend outside to man I'm in trouble. So I hear the engine turn off of my dad's work truck, the door opens, then shuts. My bedroom window was open so I could hear him getting out the truck than entering the house. The thumping of his work boots knocking on the hollow floor as he walks the hallway and down to my parents room. I hear him wake up my mother as the two of them begin to argue I say to myself man I really fucked up bad. The arguing got louder and louder my dad yelling, my mother screaming, then my door bursts open as my friend and I are literally shitting our self. My dad yells Jacob get your ass out here now follow me. So I follow him out my bedroom, down the hallway, and out the front door. He begins to tell me how mad and disappointed he is in me and that I could of put not only myself but my friend in danger as well. How this little selfish act that I just pulled, anything could have happened, that we could have been seriously hurt. He continued to yell at my mother asking her why she was sleeping instead of watching us and cooking, that he works hard to protect his family and this is what he has to come home to nothing but disrespect. Now I knew my father met well but he was just way to over protective. He was always paranoid for no reason he always felt like someone or something was out to get him. That you need to always be on the look out, that nobody was safe. I don't know he was on alcoholic, he drank a lot, but overall he was a good father to me and a good husband to my mother. He would take my friend and I fishing a lot and he would read to me a lot even though he wasn't the most educated man so naturally as I got older my reading skills would increase more and more. I was placed in all honors classes all throughout my schooling and this made other kids pick on me and my friend a lot. My father would always tell me to be something better than him and most importantly to leave Aberdeen. So I remember that night my father got really upset about what my friend and I had done, he had told my friend to leave and me to go to my room that I was grounded. My mother thought that he was overreacting but there was nothing that she could say or do about it. So I went to my room crying I was so upset that my father was upset. You see I love my father very much he is my idol and I never lied to him much less went against anything he ever said or did and I never wanted to hurt my dad. So as I'm sitting in my room my father comes in and sits down and tells me "Jacob look I love you more than anything" do you know what I would do if I lost you? I would lose it, I would go nuts you are my world. Look son I'm sorry for yelling at you and your mother ok? Do you forgive me? I replied "It's ok dad I understand I forgive you." He replied "ok I love you Jacob, now clean up and get ready for dinner as he gets up to leave the room and out the door he says "oh yeah and I hope your shot has improved you're going to show me it later after dinner for trying to be a big man laughing." I replied laughing back "ok dad I've gotten better." My dad replied ok that's good just remember you can't beat me though laughing. I replied "ok will see laughing back." Then he turned around walked up to me and kissed me on my forehead and told me to get ready and cleaned up for dinner that he loved me and that he would be right back. That would be the last time that I saw my father alive. My mother told me that he was going across the street to the bar like he would always do after work and just before dinner time. Only on this particular night on his way back from the bar crossing the road a man driving a white 1979 Cadillac hit my father dead on killing him instantly dead on site. I remember the police report saying that my father's blood alcohol level was so high that they weren't sure how he didn't drop dead at the bar instead of outside of it. Anyways do to the fact that my father was intoxicated while leaving the bar and crossing the road plus the fact that this man with the white 1979 Cadillac Theodore Banks was a rich and wealthy man on what they called a technicality back then Theodore Banks walked as if my father wasn't the victim that lost his life. Granted my father was drunk but this man still killed him point blank drunk or not. Now at 13 years old I remember sitting in that courtroom with my mother watching her cry and feeling powerless yet watching this Theodore show no remorse what so ever for what he had done to my father. For this and this reason alone is why I put my hoop dreams aside and became a defense attorney and decided to practice law so that this type of injustice could never happen again. I can remember how happy Theodore was at the final hearing Mr. Banks and his lawyer celebrating, painting a picture of my poor hardworking father to be this monster of a man, a drunk who was better off the streets so rich people like Mr. Banks could make a better living. My mother didn't have a lot of money so we couldn't hire a decent lawyer, so the guy we got could careless for what he was being paid weather justice was served or not. I remember Banks almost smiling at me in the courtroom it made me sick to my stomach. The day of my father's funeral there wasn't even enough money to put down a headstone for him. My mother got a job as a waitress at a local diner to make ends meet and people where very supportive in the community and the Neighborhood. At the steel mill where my father worked at a few of the guys chipped in and donated money to help with the funeral costs. I stayed in the books just like my father always told me to do and by High School I was studying law. I would intern at law offices as much as possible, I wanted as much knowledge and information as I could possibly get. I was hungry and thirst for knowledge and I didn't want to be just another lawyer I wanted to be the absolute best. But not just to win but to help protect injustice like this from happening because it was done to my father and I couldn't do anything to help him but I damn sure can help him by helping others. I can remember one time sitting in a diner I must of been about 18 or 19 at the time and out of nowhere who do I see? Theodore Banks the man who killed my father. Shit five years later I never forgot this man's face, now mind you he must of been 60 or so but he still looked the same to me. He walked through them double doors and looked to his right and there I was Jacob Cass Jr. He is looking dead right at me right into my eyes and begins walking over towards me as my heart is racing because I don't know what I want to do? Should I just sit there and see what he has to say? Should I knock him out? Should I get up and leave? Or should I conduct myself like a gentleman? Fuck that a lawyer in training that is? As he gets closer and closer I could feel my face getting hotter and hotter. Then he gets to me and says "Are you Jacob Cass's boy?" I replied "yes I am" Mr. Banks replied I thought you looked familiar. Well listen I never got a chance to tell you how sorry that I am about your father I never met to hurt him. I replied "Hurt him?" you mean "Kill him?" Mr. Banks replied umm so I hear your studying law now that is great? I bet your father would be proud of you. You look just like him well from the papers that is. Gosh you are all grown up now I remember you in that courtroom so young looking. As he politely sits down at my table I ask Mr. Banks is there something that I can help you with? Mr. Banks replied "Oh umm no I just simply wanting to give you my deepest condolences. I replied thank you after 5 years absolutely appreciate it. Mr. Banks replied I am sorry I gave my condolences to your mother years ago. I replied stay away from me and my mother do you understand me? Mr. Banks replied I am sorry well I will get going now I just simply wanted to say that I am sorry for your loss and again I never meant it also to tell you congratulations on pursuing law. That is a good thing but always remember that "sometimes when you think that you are fucking them, they really are fucking you" you know what I mean? I replied "yeah whatever are we done here?" Mr. Banks replied "yeah ok take care" I replied "same to you". I said to myself how the fuck did he even know that I was studying law? And what the fuck was that comment that he made about? Anyways later that day I remember going home and telling my mother about my run in with Mr. Banks at the diner. My mother was very upset and told me to stay away from him i told her that he knew about me pursuing law how would he know that? My mother replied Aberdeen is small Jacob you know everybody knows everything around here. I said to myself hey maybe she was right. Anyways I blew through High School like it was nothing and before you knew it I was on to damn near Collage with many opportunities locally but my father always wanted me to leave Aberdeen. I said to myself although I want to follow his dreams for me I have my own to fulfill and leaving Aberdeen just wasn't going to cut it for me. I always wanted to be a Georgetown Hoya but as I got older I became obsessed with something bigger and that was law. The where for me was anywhere but I wasn't leaving Aberdeen for nothing. But then I got an external scholarship at UCLA School of Law and the opportunity was great but I had never been that far away from home before. Hell I had never really been outside of Aberdeen, I never been away from family. My mother would be all by herself it was just a really rough decision to make should I stay in Aberdeen or jump on this great opportunity and go to California? I knew this was a great opportunity to further my career. I mean shit it was California and to me California was Hollywood and if I wanted to be a great lawyer why not start there right? So try telling that to my mother who thought the big city of Los Angeles was filled with crime, drugs, and nothing positive for a country guy like me. I told her that was perfect because we would bring in a lot of clients if California is really as bad as she thinks it is. My mother replied that is great for your career and work I completely understand that but it's not good for my child my only one at that do you understand? I replied I do understand mom but you also have to understand that I am not a child anymore. I told her mom pop always wanted me to get out of Aberdeen now I think Los Angeles could use a good attorney such as myself don't you agree? My mother replied so could Aberdeen Jacob. I think the thought of being alone scared her a lot because I was all she had left. I told her that if I go to California once I get settled in and get my own place off of campus that I would fly her out there. As much as she hated the idea of me having to leave she knew that it was a great opportunity for me. I remember the day she gave me her blessings to go I think we both cried that day. She picked me up from Aberdeen high School and had my scholarship letter in her hand. When I got into the car and she looked at me and says "go Jacob" I am sorry for trying to stop you from going that was very selfish of me. I am very proud of you and I want you to go and fulfill your dreams because you make me proud everyday and I know that your father is proud of you So go be great I love you son. With tears rolling down her face as they began to fall down from mine as well I replied "Thank you mom" I love you so much and I promise dad's death won't go in vain I will make you both proud and as soon as I get settled in I will fly you out. My mother replied we are already proud of you Jacob. Then before you knew it was graduation time at Aberdeen High School and i made it on that stage and seeing how happy my mother was in that crowd made it all worth it. That was a dream of hers as all parents was to see her son or daughter graduate from high school cap and gown and all. Now months before leaving for California i was still interning at the same firm that i had been all throughout high school which was called Parker&Parker. They were very happy for me and for a graduation present and a going away present they gave me the best gift of all better than anything i could ever ask for. They went down to Fern Hill Cemetary personally and paid for a head stone for my father's grave site. I was speechless I couldn't believe it. When I told my mother she was in tears she was so grateful, she felt that now my father could rest somewhat peacefully. Now when it was time to leave Aberdeen for probably the first time in my life that I can remember for Los Angeles California I was in mixed feelings. Because on one hand I am leaving which is a new expirence all in itself but i've never been to Cali and I don't know how the people are there and what to expect at the campus. But on the hand it would be difficult having to leave my mother, my biggest supporter throughout my entire life good or bad she was always there for me but now in California I am going to be all alone by myself. So the day I was leaving for California I said goodbye to Aberdeen and we headed for Bowerman airport. In the car all I could think about was how UCLA going to be? How is California going to be? I could tell that my mother was fighting back tears as was I. Now during the ride there my mother just basically spoke to me about staying focused, no parties, no drugs, no alcohol, stay the same, stay the same, stay in law school and stay true to myself. Don't let the life stye of law and California get to me and let it change me. I told her that it wouldn't and that it couldn't I am a third generation Cass and that I was going to make her and my father proud of me. I remember getting to the airport and it finally sunk it that I was leaving Aberdeen for good and probably wouldn't see it or my mother for a long time. I told my mother as we both shed tears that I would call her every single day just to check up on her and for her to know that I was ok and before you knew it I was off to LAX. On the plane to Los Angeles I mostly listen to music and looked up local attorney offices near by campus that I could work for or intern for. But I just couldn't see myself interning anymore because I knew eventually I was going to need money a lot of money you know what I mean? Well before you knew it I would hear the piolet announcing on the speaker "now landing at LAX Los Angeles airport" now when I landed after getting my luggage I got a cab and headed straight to UCLA. In the cab I could remember everything looking so much different out here than from back home. This was California the people looked different it was like another planet it was way different from Aberdeen everybody out here looked rich and fancy very classy. Man back home everyone is country dressed in jeans and a T-shirt or hunting gear or fishing gear. When we finally pulled up to the campus all I could say was "oh my god" this campus is huge I mean I knew UCLA would be big but not at all quite like this. Man I had no idea where to go i had the address to the campus where I was suppose to be at but when the cab driver asked me what part of the campus are you looking for? I have no idea where to go so I had the cab driver just drop me off and I walked around campus and asked people where was I suppose to go? This is when i met Blake. Blake was a shy quiet white guy going here for medical school he showed me where the main office was and he and i would become friends throughout my time at UCLA. Now my roommate on the other hand that was a whole other story he was an asshole and straight up dick head from the minute i met him. I mean after administration took care of me and everything i was walked to my room. But this guy Blake if it wasn't for him my first day would have been even more hell than it was about to be. So when i get to my dorm room put the key in the door this guy swings open the door giving me the dirtest look and says "who the fuck are you?" please tell me that you are not my roommate? As I am thinking to myself what an asshole this guy is. He opens the door wearing only a pair of boxer briefs and a pair of socks blasting music very loud. I replied my name is Jacob and yes I believe I am your new roommate. He replied good my name is Dennis and this is my world so as long as you don't fuck off we will get along just fine. I replied ok I really don't know what that means? Dennis replied you will find out now move out of my way as Blake and I were standing in the door way we both moved and Dennis leaves. Now I could tell rooming with him was going to be a problem I mean this fucking guy really thought that he could do what he wanted and treat people any type of way he felt he could. So life at UCLA sucked it really did class didn't but rooming with Dennis did. My classes id fly through them like it was nothing I knew law like the back of my head because I was so passionate about it and I didn't want to see what happened to my father happen to anybody else ever again. I mean id see things like that or similar to that happen and people, killers, walk because their public defender or cheap ass lawyer let them walk but not me not on my watch. Every morning I would call my mother first thing I do when I wake up, and once before bed. God I miss her she would always ask me how law school was going? I'd tell her it was great I didn't want to upset her with telling her about my asshole roommate. I missed mom and Aberdeen I had no social life as like back home because I felt having fun chilling, parting, hanging out was for people who feel they have made it in life they act like they are already home. Like they have already crossed the finish line and to me I just wasn't there yet but i'll celebrate when i've made it. When I am at the top of the mountain they can all party ill study. Anyways back to asshole Dennis, first off i'd have exams and this guy would be parting all hours of the night blasting music. He always kept his side of the room a mess, he was funky just a dirty motherfucker. I often fanticized about whooping his ass but then i'd come back to reality and look at his massive 6 foot 7 frame and build and keep my opinions to myself. Hell laugh all you want this guy was huge though so this disrespect and asshole bullshit went on for two out of my four years at UCLA law School up until two major events changed all that. Man I had enough of Dennis and expressed this to my good friend Blake a lot pretty much every day for two years. But Blake had been working off campus at some shoe store out in the valley and decided that we should just move off of campus together that he knew of a nice cheap affordable one bedroom close nearby campus. He told me that he would buy a pull out couch so that i would have a bed and jokingly told me that i wouldn't need the bedroom because I have no friends but him and no girlfriend and no social life what so ever. Blake would often tease me and tell me that I jerk off to law school that law was my woman. Shit I was about 20 or 21 and still a virgin, yep believe it or not and it wasn't that I wasn't good looking or anything like that I guess I just never made time for all that social mingling life although there was this one girl a beautiful blonde girl I use to see her a lot around campus. I use to fine myself staring at her and often id see her staring back but I never built up the balls or courage to talk to her. Who was I kidding? She was way out of my league. She was very beautiful, a blonde, hazel eyes, red boned, thick, just goregous she looked mixed but hell I am a bum with nothing to offer her. So Blake teased me a lot he was like a little brother to me and looked out a lot. I told him that once I get on my feet I would pay him back. He would tell me that my friendship was payment enough that when I become the biggest top attorney around just too simply remember him. So at about the two year mark of college Blake and I moved into his place with him still going to medical school not law anymore but I was still in law school. Then about two weeks of us living here off campus and me sleeping on the couch one day I get a call from my former employer back in Aberdeen from the law firm Parker and Parker where i was an intern at giving me unbelievably great news. I was told that since i put in two years of interning and being an apprentice at Parker and Parker that they were going to talk to UCLA and instead of me getting my bachlors degree in 4 years I can get it in 3 and in the meantime I will be working at a law firm they got me into called Almonds and Almonds and this would help me pass the bar exam and get a license in the state of California because California state law says that 18 hours for 4 years you can become an attorney by appentice or interning. Now we have done 2 years of both, plus law school 2 years, so 1 more year at Almonds and Almonds I will be able to clear the bar exam to become a license attorney. This was the best news I was so happy now id be making money and could pay Blake back hell I could move I could do whatever I wanted I was so close to making my dream a reality I said to myself Almonds and Almonds here I come. Now the day i went to Almond and Almonds I met Sabastion, he told me what to do and how to do it he was the boss there. Now the top lawyer there at the time I showed up was a guy named Christian. Sabastion became like a mentor to me a father figure you could say of some sorts. I worked long hard nights for him and under his mentorship I became the man over night at this law firm. I had no license yet but in just six months of being here I brought a lot of cases to the company making Christian look even better. Man I did it all over there i answered phones, fixed paper work, mailed paper work, arranged meetings, brought in clients, I was so good that I thought by the time I took my exam that I would be partner for sure. You would think that Christian would like me, appreciate me, but instead me doing so good made him dislike me because he knew that I was coming for his spot. In school id fall asleep because of late nights at the office and plus I knew all this shit they were trying to teach. Hell at times I felt like I should be teaching the class and because of this now Mr. Ferguson my favorite teacher thinks I have an attitude or some kind of chip on my shoulders when all I want to do is win and help others. At times it seemed like the only person who really understood me was my mom and Sabastion. My mother would often tell me to calm down and let god do his job. I wanted to become an attorney more than anything i could taste it, I could feel it, I was so close. Then six months later it was now time for me legally to take the bar exam and boy was I nervous yet so excited and when it was all said and done I passed the bar. Yep all my hard work, all my dedication, my blood, my sweat, and my tears, you now could finally call me Defense Attorney Jacob G. Cass III and i represent Almonds and Almonds with my bachlors degree from the university of UCLA. When i called my mother and told her the good news she cried so much and told me how proud she was of me. I could hear her yell to her friends in the background "you hear that you all?" "my baby boy, my son is a lawyer you all" living out in California yep my baby boy did it. She replied Jacob your father is smiling down on you in heaven I know he is so proud of you we all are. I replied thank you but mom I have another surprise for you. My mother replied what's that baby? I replied I am getting my own place and I am going to fly you out for my graduation. She was so happy she replied Jacob I can't wait I am so happy for you son I love you very much. I replied I love you too mom but I have to go I will speak to you soon. She replied ok son I love you call me later. I replied I will love you too mom and I hung up. But now I just really needed to get my own place and break the news to Blake that I was leaving. When I told Blake he was happy for me but expressed several times how he wanted me to stay living with him so breaking the news to him wouldn't be easy. When it was time to break the news to Blake he wasn't happy like I thought he would be but he did understand. He thought that I was moving a bit too fast and thought that I should stay awhile longer at his place at least a few more months. But I told him that I wanted my own place that living with him has been fun that I learned a lot from him because of Blake I learned how to navagate the campus of UCLA he made my time there better. Times when I was down and wanted to give up or go back home it was Blake that had my back but for him I guess me leaving was bitter sweet because me leaving UCLA, our place, and working at Almonds and Almonds id have less and less time to talk with him. Man Sabastion bought me a couple of suits and ties and I was his right handman striaght out of law school living my dream and then it happened. Probably the biggest case since the Simpson trial hits my desk. A drunk driver hits and kills some random kids 18 year old son but this drunk driver wasn't your avarage person it was none other then Kayshawn James one of if not the biggest basketball player in the world. This guy was hailed as the Michael Jordan of basketball today and I said to myself "hell yeah" this was it this was the case I needed to not only help but to become the man. Man I loved Kayshawn James i've been a fan of his for years and it would be sad to see him in jail but bet your ass that's where he is headed and i will make sure of it. You see Kayshawn James is a hell of an athlete and an ispiration to the world as was O.J. but celebrity or not justice has to be served. It's not ok that just because you have more money and you are always on the television you can just walk. I said to myself "fuck that" what's right is right and what's wrong is wrong celebrities are human to just like us. This family lost their 18 year old son to a drunk driver that is my defense they're will be to tell you that Kayshawn James made a mistake Well you damn right he did and I will see that he pays for it to. You see lawyers we are told to not be biased never care about who is guilty or not just as long as they pay and you always win no matter what it takes. That is the reality of it people but not for me and you all already know why. Now immediately I went to Sabastion's office and told him we are on this I want to represent the Johnson family we are taking James down. Sabastion replied Jacob you come in here to tell me you want to represent the victim? I would think the safe win would be backing James don't you think? This is huge Jacob we could lose. I replied no Sabastion you know why I want to represent the Johnsons and with all due respect i got this and you can count on me that James won't walk not while I am breathing and on this case. Sabastion replied his pockets are heavy have you contacted Mr. Johnson yet? I replied no but I am on it. Sabastion replied you sure you want this Jacob? This is career making or breaking here you know that right? I replied exactly man this was huge Fox, CNN, you name it and everybody began to watch it all unfold on national television "Superstar ball player involved in a hit and run accident that leaves an 18 year old dead." Now as I am preparing to contact Mr. Johnson Sabastion comes into my office and tells me that Christian wants the case and that he and i should work together on this. I replied look Sabastion you believed in me that is why I am here right? Sabastion replied yes of course i do Jacob. I replied ok and how many cases have you put Christian on the whole time that he has been here for? Sabastion replied a lot why? I replied and you pretty much had to groom him into the lawyer that he is today and I take nothing from him he is great but I believe that this is my time to shine the hot young fresh attorney straight out of law school. look I am quick, I am sharp, and you know this otherwise you wouldn't have invested your time in me. The point I am trying to make is a hit and run Sabastion really? This case is what i've busted my ass for years for this is the one and if he walks i will be kicking myself in the ass for not being able to help this family. Look on my father's name Sabastion i need this please? But me and me only in that courtroom no offense to Christian but I need this one he can help give advise and what not but I am in the driver's seat on this one ok? Sabastion replied ok Jacob don't fuck this up it's your ass on the line you better bring it home and you're going to have to explain this to Christian yourself. I replied "will do" I wouldn't have it any other way boss. Now the first thing I needed to do was to get in contact with Mr. Johnson so I gave him a call but nobody answered so I left a message that went like this "hello Mr. and Mrs. Johnson I am deeply sorry for your loss. I'm calling to see if you have seeked councel yet regarding your loss? My name is Jacob G. Cass III and I am a defense attorney, I represent the law firm of Almonds and Almonds and I would love to represent you all in this matter and bring you some closure by putting Kayshawn James behind bars please give me a call back at your earliest convenience thank you and my god bless. Now

I needed to speak with Christian regarding the case matter. You see I don't even have the case yet but I want to make sure that he doesn't contact them to try and steal this from me because if they don't have counsel yet I will get them this is my job it's what I do this case is mine. So when I knocked on Christian's door to speak to him he told me to come in. So immediately I get right into it and do you know what this guy has the nerve to say to me? he says Jacob first off for you to not ask but to tell Sabastion that you are taking this case is disrespectful to him. After all that he has done for you, you ask him not tell him. Second off if this case should go to anybody it should go to me not you, for christ sake you haven't even worked a case before what makes you think that you could win a case of this magnitude? Third you're helping the losing side not the winning side any lawyer can tell you that the chances of the court prosecuting Kayshawn James is slim to fucking none but then again your Jacob Cass right? This fucking cocksucker had the balls to talk to me like I was fucking stupid or something. So I replied by saying "wow" well first off I asked Sabastion if I could have this case. Second I didn't come in here to get your advise or approval I came in here to tell you that I am going for this case and for you not to ask Sabastion he told me to speak to you myself so here I am. Third I am not going for the losing side the Johnson's will win and I will make sure of that but its attorney's just like you that let scum like James walk away in their celebrity. Christian replied good luck Jacob I won't stand in your way trust me when this all explodes in your face I want absolutely no part of it. We are done now so please let yourself out and close my door behind you please. I replied you are only making me look that much better bye.

Can you believe this guy? So I turned around and I left. The next day I must of called Mr. Johnson about 3 more times only to keep getting their answering machine. So I said to myself it was time for me to make contact yep you heard that right. I was hungry and needed this case so another attorney rule is this if you can't reach them by phone, email, letters, nothing then it is time to make contact by getting there address and going over to their place of residence. Now they lived locally in down town Los Angeles but in a rough neighborhood called Compton. Now I had never been there before but I am familiar with NWA and all my favorite rappers that grew up there. So I was actually excited to go there and see it. So I took maybe a 20 or 30 minute drive out there after getting the address from Sabastion. Now when i got out there I mean from the minute I pulled onto their street there were kids on each sides of my car looking in it. I had my windows rolled down and they were yelling "Cop" I guess they thought I was a cop I was driving a company car as I still hadn't had my own or my own place yet. Once I got to the Johnson's place I can admit I was a bit nervous because I had no idea how to approach this law school prepares you for the courtroom and the system but not this. I remember knocking on the door wearing a nice suit and tie sharp dress shoes smelling really good no cheap shit looking and feeling like a million bucks and then Mr. Johnson answers the door i know this because he was all over the papers. He says hello? I replied hello Mr. Johnson? He replied yes who are you? I told the cops everything already. I replied oh no Sir I am not a cop my name is Jacob G. Cass III Sir I am an attorney for Almonds and Almonds as i give him my business card. He replied you look awfully young to be an attorney son how old are you? I replied I will be 25 in May Sir. He replied yeah you look very young. Anyways Mr. Cass is it? My family and I are very poor and I really have no money to pay for an attorney so I am sorry that you drove over here and I thank you for trying to help us. Now here is where I decided to do something that almost got me fired. I replied "no no" trouble at all but Mr. Johnson what if I told you that I would like to take your case for free? Mr. Johnson replied for free? I replied "yes for free" Mr. Johnson replied son ain't nothing in this world for free what is your angle Mr. Cass? What do you have going on? I replied nothing no angle sir if you can just let me in for 10 minutes that's all I ask I can explain i promise you? Mr. Johnson replied ok Cass you got 10 minutes because I'm curious to know what attorney would take on a case for nothing I've never heard of anything like that before. I replied I understand sir I will explain my position in the matter. So Mr. Johnson invited me into his home he escorted me into their living room area and there sat his elderly wife in a lazy boy chair. Mr. Johnson then introduced me to his wife Mrs. Johnson and asked me to take a seat which I did. I told them both how deeply sorry that I was for their loss. So Mr. Johnson then asked me why was I willing to represent them for free? I replied well Mr. Johnson it is simple you're a hardworking man such as myself you have worked for the city for years you adopted a child your wife also very hardworking you are a blue collar family good hardworking people. I feel like i can identify with you all as I am myself. I don't even have my own apartment yet, I live with a friend, i've never worked a court case before, I am fresh out of law school. But the catch is that your son was struck by a car now had an average person such as you or myself had been driving this vehicle we would go straight to jail right or wrong? But Kayshawn James is arguably the best basketball player in the world since Jordan and because of this he is still a free man headed to trial. This to me is unexceptable he should be in jail like the average person the problem is that money talks and James has a lot of it you all don't but how is this fare? The answer is that it's not. Now 9 times out of 10 you will be given a public defender we call them public pretenders who could care less about the case or the matter because they are getting a paycheck to represent you regardless or might get one who will cop a plea deal get you a little money and James gets a slap on the wrist I say "NO" this is about a life that was taken entirely to soon be a drunk driver celebrity or not broke or wealthy. You all deserve justice not cash and he deserves to be punished not able to write a check and life goes on while you both mourn over your loss. Now I am willing to represent you both for free because I have also lost my father to a drunk driver when I was a kid but this rich and wealthy man walked because he simply had money and my family didn't and nobody cared so we lost everything. So I told myself that I would never allow something like this to ever happen to anyone again but in order to ensure that what did I do? Well to change the law you have to practice and know the law so I studied my ass off middle, high, and College and dedicated my life to becoming a lawyer, This was my calling this tragic incident right here. You see I believe god brought me to the both of you because my father didn't get justice because there was nobody like me to help us but you all have me to help you. I give my word to you both Mr. and Mrs. Johnson that as long as there is air in my lungs justice will be served for your child Brandon you have my word. Mr. Johnson replied I am very sorry young man for your loss as well and now I can see why you are so eager to help us and I appreciate that young man. Well it seems as if I can't refuse the offer but Mr. Cass this is a very high profile case and you did mention before that this would be in fact your very first case that doesn't have me to convinced that you can or will win this case. I replied and I completely agree with you and see your point however with taking your chances with a free lawyer as appose to a public defender who don't care or a plea deal or you put up the money for a good guarantee attorney what do you really have to lose? Plus you know that i am young, ambitious, and this case means something to me personally as well I say what do you have to lose Mr. Johnson? Mr. Johnson replied umm I suppose your right, you talk a good game Cass I give you that I just hope your half as good as you say you are son. I replied I am that good and more so do we have ourselves a deal here? Mr. Johnson looked over at his wife while she looked back at him nodding her head yes Mr. Johnson replied you promised us justice Mr. Cass and that is exactly what I expect you hear me? I replied "say no more" and we shook hands. Now Mr. Johnson asked what's next? I replied well I need you to come down to my office sometime tomorrow before 5 pm and will go over some paper work for you to sign and after that we will get this ball rolling. Mr. Johnson replied ok Mr. Cass sounds good I will see you tomorrow then possibly after 1 we have church to go to. I replied ok it was a pleasure meeting you both Mr. and Mrs. Johnson and trust me you both are in good hands I promise you that. See you both tomorrow and once again I am very sorry for your loss and if there is anything else I can do to help the both of you I don't care what time of the day it is don't hesistate to call me ok. They both replied thank you Mr. Cass and may god bless. Oh my god I was so happy I got the case I am now the lead attorney for the Johnson Family this was huge this was big now I just needed to tell my boss Sabastion who I knew wasn't going to be happy with me at all I also had to tell my mother and Blake as well, Plus I still needed to find a place I said to myself tomorrow is going to be a busy day. That next morning bright and early it must of been 7 or 8 in the morning I called my mother to tell her the good news. She expressed her happiness for me but also told me to be careful because this was such a high profile case and that i would be recieving a lot of public attention. But I asured her that i was fine with it all and that not only was I going to win but that I could handle the pressure. My mother told me to priase god and to stay humble and focused that I am her son always and that she is so very proud of me but that she does worry about me being out in California. So after i got off the phone with my mother Blake came out of his room and asked me what was up? I also never mentioned to my mother that I took the case for free and that bothered me. anyways i told Blake though and for some reason he didn't look or sound happy at all for me, in fact he told me that what i did was stupid and that i might have lost my job for nothing. I was so angry when he said "for nothing" really? For nothing? I said if me losing money for trying to help this family get some fucking closure some fucking justice then i guess it was stupid. I told Blake i believe in and stand behind my decision and you and i have been through alot together and for you to say something like that to me is just nuts man. I went on to say but don't worry Blake bro i'm getting my own place as soon as possible don't worry. Blake replied Jacob you are over exsaggerating i only met that you always go by the book you should have asked Sabastion before you made the deal if it was ok. I replied their was no time. Blake you know everyone is gunning for this case everyone and it belongs to me nobody else you know how hard i worked for this bro you know that. Blake replied your right Jacob i'm sorry i only ment well i just want you to stay focused and do well this is a lot of pressure on you i can tell so sometimes you might not be thinking clearly and as your close friend since you don't have a woman or any other friends for that matter (laughing) i feel its my place to give you advice from time to time thats all. I replied laughing back thanks bro and i got this also im tired of you making fun of my personal life i'm going to kick your ass bro laughing. I tell you what if i win this case will go out partying and drinking whatever it is you people do nowadays laughing what do you say? Blake replied deal the great Jacob Cass will finally be normal their still is hope as we both laughed i replied ok well like normal this workaholic needs to get to work, So off to work i went. Now when i got to my office immediatly Sabastion comes into my office and asked me what the deal was? I told him look i know when i tell you this your going to be pissed but please Sabastion i got this you need to trust me on this one. Sabastion replied what did you do Jacob? I replied well i got the case. Sabastion replied and the part i'm not going to like is? Well they don't have money so they where closing the door in my face. Sabastion replied ok so did you set up a payment plan with them? I replied Jacob what the fuck did you do? I replied i took the initiative like you always taught me. you taught me to always do the right thing in law as long as you always win. Sabastion replied please tell me you didn't do what i think you did? I replied look Sabastion there people come from nothing they are elderly folks who are broke and just lost there son to a drunk driver so i did what i thought was the god like thing to do. I said to myself i can do something positive very positive and i offered to take the case for free. Sabashion laughing as his face turns beat red and says Jacob that was a very stupid and selfish thing of you to do but guess what its not free because it will come out of your pay win, lose, or draw, do you understand me? i replied yeah whatever we are clear, oh and another thing how in gods name is me taking a case for free selfish? That makes no sense to me because im trying to help there people? Sabastion replied no Jacob your trying to help yourself you want justice for your father not for Mr and Mrs. Johnson you want to be their attorney to bring closure to your fathers case but this isn't your fathers case this is about the Johnson family. So you through the rule book out because your losing focus Jacob already and you haven't even stepped foot in the courtroom yet. I replied Sabastion you have been like a father to me, a mentor, honestly do you think that i can't handle this? You know i'm the right person for this and yes it hits close to home but that is also why i'm the best person for it just trust me i got this. Sabastion replied just get your head out of your ass because this is the biggest case in the country and you asked for it be careful what you wish for Jacob goodluck. I replied thanks pops now can i get back to work? Or actually can i leave a little earlier today possibly around 6:00 or so because i need to meet with a realitor? Sabastion replied Jacob you have the case of the century and you want to go home early? Absolutly not no go on your lunch break or reschudle it. i replied lunch break i guess will do. So after Sabastion left i immediatly called the realitor to reschudle for my lunch break. Then i had to prepare all the paperwork for Mr and Mrs. Johnson for later on today. The work day went by very slow and everybody was happy for me and that our firm got the case it was a really big deal for the entire office because me getting the case put Almonds and Almonds on the map and it was all because of me and that felt good. Of course their is always one person that has to rain on your parade and be a hater which in this case was Christian but i didn't care he never like me ever since i came here because like i said before this was like his office he has always been the top attorney here and this case would of took him to new hights possibly even stardom but i was in his way and he didn't like that plus my relationship with Sabastion made him sick to his stomach the whole father son thing. But im sure he had that same treatment to when he was the new guy at the firm as well. So anyways around 11:50am i left early on my lunch break to go meet the realitor about this nice house i had been looking at. It was a beautiful two bedroom home with two bathrooms an office and a swimming pool all overlooking Venice beach. The price well? Well where not going to get into all that but lets just say that i have been saving every nickel and dime for along time and i deserved this so i was really sure that this is what i wanted plus it beat sleeping on Blakes couch. So as im talking to the realitor he is showing me around trying to sell the place he says to me "yeah Mr. Cass i was so siked when i found out that i might be selling to a big time attorney such as yourself." I replied what makes you think that i am big time? The realitor replied well aren't you the attorney that is going against Kayshawn James? I replied yes i am how did you know that? As he looks confused he replied well that's all their talking about on television that Attorney Jacob Cass is the lead prosecuting attorney or defense attorney something like that. He then asked me are you really going to try to put Kayshawn James in jail? I mean you don't really think he did it right? I replied yes i am. When did you see this on television? He replied it's been all over television since the news broke out this morning. I replied who released the story? The realitor replied i think TMG or something like that why? I replied what is that? The realitor replied really? Its like a news gossip site or something it even shows picturues of you leaving those peoples house and speaking with them. I replied are you kidding me with me right now? He replied no sir. He then asked me is something wrong sir? I replied no nothing at all can you excuse me for a minute though please? The realitor replied sure take your time. I then stepped outside of the home to call my boss Sabastion in confustion like what the fuck is going on? Was i being followed by reporters? What the fuck. Sabastion awnsers immediatly and says well hey there superstar? I replied Sabastion this ain't funny what is going on? He replied this is the price of fame son TMG broke the news now its all over from here congratulations. I replied i didn't ask for this. Sabastion replied oh yes you did i told you to be careful what you wish for Jacob I guess they followed you. I replied why me? Sabastion replied well Jacob word gets out it could be anybody whoever knows speaks to their friends and their friend speaks to someone else take your pick it's only going to get worse Jacob it's a high profile case get use to it son. But look will talk more when you get back I have poporitzzi here now because of you i have to go. I replied ok talk to you soon and we hung up. I said to myself fuck this is crazy. So now I go back into the house and the realitor says "ok Mr. Cass our we ready to sign some papers or what?" I replied look I tell you what I love this place but it is very pricey so can you guys make a deal with me or what? The realitor replied hmm i'm sure we could let me give my boss a call first and find out give me a minute. I replied ok you go ahead and do that I have to run I'm a very busy man as of late and pressed for time but you know how to reach me though. The realitor replied but wait Mr. Cass we can handle this now. I replied yeah ok get back to me I have to run as I'm quickly going out the door on my way to my car. So when I got back to the office it was a mad house it looked like Beyonce or something was outside of the office it was a circus. Mad poporratzz was outside snapping pictures and all this mess that by the time I pulled in my parking spot I damn near crashed from the flashing lights and what not. When I finally got out of my car it was a mob seen I had microphones shoved in my face "Attorney Cass?" "Mr. Cass?' Can we get a word? Do you really think Keyshawn James is guilty? Are you going to really put him behind bars? Man it was crazy I simply reply by saying nothing and ran from my car to the building. I didn't know what to say or how to say it so Sabastion told the press that Almonds and Almonds is handling the case but that is all that we are saying at this time. When I finally got into the building I ran straight to my office my heart was beating so fast I was nervous as fuck and sweating like crazy. I had calls from Blake, calls from my mother, but I ignored them all I had to prepare for the Johnsons I had to get focused and fast. So while I was preparing the paper work Sabastion comes into my office and says to me Jacob are you sure you can handle all of this? Cause if not Christian will take the driver's seat on this one if you want. I replied Sabastion I am getting really fed up with you second guessing and questioning me and my god given abilities to win and handle this case on my own two feet. I have already told you that I am open to suggestions from the rest of the firm but I am the leader nobody is driving but me ok? I don't want to hear about it anymore fuck. Christian then enters the office in rage as Sabastion and others hold him back and try to calm him down. He yells Cass your nothing but an ungrateful rookie a novelist punk who thinks you can talk to people anyway you want to don't you ever talk to my mentor ever like that again you fucking punk. I replied the nerve of you to walk into my motherfucking office and try to lecture me, if it wasn't for me we wouldn't have this case. If it wasn't for me Almonds and Almonds would be just another hole in the wall firm I made this place what it is today we are fucking national look outside each of your windows right now, you see all those people? They are here for me I made this shit possible Christian not you me. So do me a favor and get the fuck out of my office your just mad that even in your prime you were never as good as me and you know it and it makes you sick to your stomach well guess what Christian eat your heart out. Christian replied calmly you see Jacob it's all about you all of this but you represent us Almonds and Almonds is a team and you are part of this team. So yeah you might be better than me even in my prime as you like to think but at least win, lose, or draw I represented for the firm and the client. You you're a joke, your selfish, you see I in team but their isn't so let me be the first to wish you the best of luck out there because baby boy trust me when I tell you that you are going to need it, I am out don't ask me for any help. I replied good I never needed it are we done here? Christian replied yeah I am done. Christian then turned around and walked out the office and the rest of the firm followed except for Sabastion. He stood there and looked at me dead in my eye and said get your head out of your ass Jacob I mean it are we clear? I replied like glass we are crystal may I get back to work now? And Sabastion slammed the door shut and left. Man I said to myself do you believe the nerve of this guy? These people should be grateful that I got us where we are at, I said to myself whatever I don't need them anyways. Later on that day around 4:30pm the Johnsons showed up it was so crazy I had to meet them in the back of the building so that they wouldn't get harassed by the poporittzzi. Mr. and Mrs. Johnson had a lot of questions and that was good because I had a lot of answers to their many questions and concerns. Obviously there biggest concern were whether or not I was capable of winning and keeping focused. I assured them that while this was a high profile case that their was no better man for the job seeing as how it hits so close to home with me and my family. The second concern was the financial end which i assured them that win, lose, or draw i will pay they don't have to pay anything at all it will all come out of my pocket alone. They just couldn't believe that somebody could be so generious but they also understood why this case and doing what i was doing met so much to me. so i said so if both of you agree with what i have presented you both with the agreement that is, all left to do is sign some paper work and we go to trial. Mr and Mrs. Johnson both agreeded and just like that i Jacob G. Cass III was the lead defense attorney representing the Johnson Family and the state of California against famous basketball player Kayshawn James your favorite athelete and mine too, But hey what's right is right and what's wrong is wrong. Nevertheless this made me the most famous yet hated attorney in the world. So a few weeks went by as both sides would gather as much information as they possibly could. Now Kayshawn James is arguably the best player in professional basketball since Michael Jordan he was at a night club celebrating a championship victory this making his second. Anyways while leaving this night club after several drinks pulls out of the parking lot and runs into 18 year old Brandon Johnson killing him on the spot but instead of stopping to help he leaves and club owner and friends attempt to clean it up to help his image and brand plus help the city and team name. Now this all would have worked if i didn't take this case but like i said before and several times that what's right is right and whats wrong is wrong. So the first stage of the court case is called the "pleading stage". During this part if the defendant pleads not guilty a date will be set for a preliminary hearing or trial. Now Kayshawn plead not guilty so for the next few weeks a jury will be selected and i have to question available jurors myself, judge, in a process called voir dire "speak the truth" to determine if any juror has a personal interest in the case, a prejudice, or bias that may wrongly influence him or her as a juror I can challenge some jurors and ask the court to excuse them from the trial. There are two types of challenges. Challenges for cause and peremptory challenge. Although peremptory challenges are unlimited number of challenges for cause. Anyways once the jury was selected i was almost positive that we picked all the right people. Now by the time opening statements had to be made i looked this jury dead in the face and told them. Ladies and Gentelman of the jury Good Morning and thank you for giving the court your time. I do know that this isn't easy you all have a lot on your plate. My name is Jacob G. Cass III Attorney at law firm Almonds and Almonds here today representing the Johnson family. What you are about to hear today is how much or rather how great of an athlete Kayshawn James is and i agree. He is arguably the greatest athlete there is, he brought the championship home right here to the great city of Los Angeles. He is rich, he is famous, he has sneakers, clothing, you name it and trust me today you will hear about all of that. But what you won't hear about is Brandon Johnson the young man who lost his life at the hands of our beloved superstar. What the defense doesn't want you to hear is how it was covered up so that Mr. James could remain a star, a hero, in the public eye and trust me as hard as this is on you all it is very hard on me as well because Kayshawn is my favorite ball player believe it or not. My friends think that i am crazy for taking this case they say bro how could you get Kayshawn arrested? I tell them Kayshawn whether mistake or not should be held accountable for his own actions just like any one of us he is human just like us. Why does money make Mr. James any better than us? Ask yourself this, if either one of you hit someone with a car than tried to cover it up would they hold a trial for either one of you? Or would you be locked up on the spot? Brandon has been dead a month now and no arrest has even been really made kayshawn is out on bail. Still living his life while Mr and Mrs. Johnson mourn the lost of brandon. Point is superstar or not we all bleed the same and as much as we would hate to have to do it or see it what's right is right and what's wrong is wrong and justice needs to be served. I will present you with all the evidence look within your hearts and ask yourself do i want to let this man walk just because he is a great ball player? Please give this family the closure that they so rightfully deserve. Thank you thats all i ask please. They were hooked i was convinced that the jury couldn't see this any other possible way but boy was i wrong and in the fight of my career. I was wrong in thinking that the public could see Kayshawn as a murderer. Because the general public loved and adored this man practically worshipped the ground that he walks on. So the media hated me and loved me at the same time. Hell time magazine called me the "Attorney they love to hate" but i realized throughout the trial that i didn't have to feed into the media my job was to convince 12 people the jury not the rest of the world that is what Sabastion taught me so that is what i did. After Kayshawn's defense team spoke their opening statements it was pretty clear that they were using his fame and celebrity to help get him out of this situation and once again the media was eating it up. But i feel that the jury was 50/50 so i needed to present them with hard hitting evidence and do what i do best and that is making people look and feel stupid and backed into a corner. So next part of the trial was presentation of the evidence and testimony of the witness. The first person i brought to the stand was the club manager of the Aces this was the club that Kayshawn was attending the night of the incident Mr. Doug "G-Low" Harris. I said Good Morning Mr. Harris. Mr. Harris replied Good Morning Sir. I replied so Mr. Harris you are the club manager correct? He replied yes i am that is correct. I replied how long have you been the manager of the club Aces for? Mr. Harris replied about 5 years. I replied is it 5 years or about 5 years? Are you unsure? Mr. Harris replied no it is 5 years. I replied ok thank you for clearing that up for us. Now in your time your 5 year time that is you have been able to meet a lot of celebrities i assume right? Mr. Harris replied yes that is one of the very many perks of the job. I replied yes must be fun, and is one of those celebrities none other than basketball superstar Kayshawn James? Mr. Harris replied yes Kayshawn is my good friend i love him, i'd do anything for him, he is a legend, a great man in the community, and has done a lot for not just myself, but the city of Los Angeles too, he is like a brother to me. i replied yes that is great he sounds like a stand up guy to me can you do me a favor and point to him if you recognize or see him in the courtroom right now. Mr. Harris replied yeah there goes my homie right there. I replied yes that is him well Mr. Harris you run the club so it's safe to say that you were at the club the night of the incident correct? Mr. Harris replied yes I was there that night but I didn't see the incident. I replied Mr. Harris I didn't ask you if you saw it I simply asked if you were at the club the night of the incident? Mr. Harris replied yes I told you I was ok. Mr. Harris what time did you arrive at the club that night? Mr. Harris replied around 9 or 10pm that night. I replied ok you told the police 9:30pm so will stick with that. The incident took place at 11:00pm you know what I do find funny though Mr. Harris? Mr. Harris replied know what is funny sir? I replied the fact that every single night day after day, year after year, month after month, the Aces has surveillance cameras turned on but on this particular night the night after the championship game when security should be at its all time best the tightest the Aces decided not to record anything that night doesn't that seem funny or strange to you Mr. Harris? Mr. Harris replied well there was a malfunction with the cameras so we couldn't use them on that night. I replied what was wrong with them? Mr. Harris replied they wouldn't record for some reason. I replied ok so don't you think you should have called a repair man or someone to fix it before opening the club given the event being held that night? Mr. Harris replied I suppose so but everyone was running around like a chicken with no head on nobody was prepared or organized staff was nervous and it was just a mess. I replied ok so as the manager it was your job to handle these matters why didn't you take charge and command your troops so to speak? Mr. Harris replied I should of but I had so much weight on my shoulders and I guess I dropped the ball a bit. I replied just a bit? Come on? a bit is an understatement more like a lot someone lost their life on that night Mr. Harris due to your lack of leadership. I replied so Kayshawn James is reported to be leaving your club at 10:50pm he is then spotted speaking to you at 10:55pm just before he gets into his suv. Then he backs out and driving drunk and while he pulls out the parking spot drives fast through the lot and runs straight into Brandon Johnson killing him on the spot. Now here is where it gets funny someone in the parking lot called the police and said it was Kayshawn James driving in the suv and possibly has a video recording on their phone. You then called the police at 11:45pm it took you 45 minutes almost an hour to dial 911 while this poor kid is dying you then waited for your superstar friend to get out of dodge to protect him the friend you mentioned earlier that you would do anything for. Objection your honor Mr. Cass is clearly badgering the witness. Sustained Mr. Cass get to the point and make it fast the judge replied. I replied sorry your honor why Mr. Harris why did it take you 45 minutes to call the police? Mr. Harris replied because like I told you before I wasn't there when it happened I was inside the club and by the time everything happened I ran outside got everyone out of the parking lot and then called 911 they then took a while to get to the club that is why sir. I feel so bad for that kid I really do man. I replied and the witness who saw you speaking to Kayshawn just minutes before it happened? Mr. Harris replied that is a lie sir. I replied no further questions at this time your honor. Man I needed the video without that I had nothing and Attorney Frank Parks Kayshawn's lawyer knew it too. So my next witness was Tina Clark the first 911 caller who said she saw Kayshawn James driving the suv that hit Brandon Johnson. Good Morning Mrs. Clark and I want to say thank you for your bravery I'm sure what you witnessed was very traumatic and it was very brave of you to call 911 after what you had witnessed but even braver to come to court and to testify under oath before this jury. So once again on behalf of myself and the Johnson family I'd like to say thank you. Ms. Clark replied you are welcome. I replied now Mrs. Clark do you watch basketball on television? Mrs. Clark replied no I don't but my boyfriend does. I replied I see, so how do you know who kayshawn James is? Ms. Clark replied who doesn't? Everyone knows who Kayshawn James is, that is my husband's favorite basketball player. That is all he ever talks about Kayshawn this and Kayshawn that. He is like a god to him or something like that he is obsessed with him. I replied well it sounds like it to me. As the jury laughs, so with that being said you would recognize Kayshawn in a crowd of people yes? Mrs. Clark replied of course I would. I replied did you get to meet Kayshawn that night? Mrs. Clark replied no but my husband tried to but wasn't able to. I replied why was that? Mrs. Clark replied because the Aces was packed that night it was the championship celebration you were lucky if you even got in the club let alone meet Kayshawn. I replied interesting, can you point out Kayshawn James to me? Is he in this courtroom right now? Ms. Clark replied yes that is him right there. I replied ok can you tell us what you witnessed on the night of the incident at 11:00pm? Ms. Clark replied Kayshawn ran into this young black male crossing the street on the sidewalk. It scared me half to death he was drunk and driving so fast through that parking lot. I replied how do you know that he was drunk Mrs. Clark? Mrs. Clark replied because he could barely walk he was stumbling all the way to the truck he shouldn't have even been driving. I replied and you are 100% positive that it was Kayshawn James the man sitting in this courtroom right now? I remind you that you are under oath Mrs. Clark so I ask again are you 100% sure that the man you saw get into this black suv was none other than Superstar point guard for the Los Angeles Shooters Mr. Kayshawn James? Mrs. Clark replied 100% without a doubt sure it was him. I replied thank you Mrs.

Clark no further questions your honor. Now listen to Mr. Frank Parks and his opening statements aka his crack at the jury. Good morning to the court. My name is Attorney Frank Parks and I am a longtime friend and attorney to Mr. James and his family. I ask the jury to please listen carefully to all the "Facts" that I will be presenting to you with throughout the course of this trial. Attorney Jacob Cass is good, he is young, he is hungry, he is ambitious, that he is. But he is at a conflict with himself and his personal life as well. You see for him this isn't about my client, for him this isn't about poor young Brandon Johnson or his family. No this is about Jacob Cass's personal ego and his demons and that is very unfair to my client. So yes I will say that my client Kayshawn James is a scholar but that is a "Fact" ladies and gentleman of the jury. Did my client grow up in the rough borough of Brooklyn New York City? Yes that is a "Fact" did my client go through Elementary School, Middle School, High School, and become scouted by 5 different Colleges before becoming the number 1 draft pick and the youngest ever by the University of UCLA the same college might I add that Attorney Cass attended? Yes those are all "Facts" ladies and gentleman of the jury. Did my client bring the Los Angeles Shooters to the Finals and win us the world championship game in his first year as a professional athlete? Yes that is a "Fact". Was my client the first string in Middle and High School? Did my client bring Championships to every team he ever played for? Does my client give back to the community in his many charitable organizations? Ladies and gentleman of the jury yes because these are all "Facts" this is public information people google it and you will find it for yourself but you know what you won't find? You won't find any violent history from my client not a single one and I remind you he grew up in east New York, Brooklyn a black male surviving in them Brooklyn streets and becoming arguably the greatest basketball player of all time. Ladies and gentleman of the jury that is very rare almost unheard of and you can also google that for those of you not familiar with Brooklyn, New York it is also public information. Ladies and gentleman of the jury my client is a hero, a success story, not a murderer, thank you for your time. Your honor at this time I'd like to bring to the witness stand Mr. Doug Harris. I replied your honor may I approach the bench? The judge replied make it fast Mr. Cass. I replied I will your honor. The judge replied come on up. I replied your honor Mr. Parks implying that I am incapable of doing my job do to conflict of interest is dead wrong this has nothing to do with my father sir. Mr. Parks replied true but I do have the right to let the jury know though your honor. The judge replied he does Mr. Cass and further more you are lucky that you were even appointed to council in the first place. I replied well I want a motion to deny and disregard the jury of what they just heard your honor. The judge replied motion denied Attorney Cass you are dismissed. I said to myself I hope the jury isn't buying this superstar bullshit. Anyways now Attorney Parks has Doug Harris on the stand and says Good Morning Sir. Mr. Parks continued look I am not going to tap dance around questions like Attorney Cass I am going to get straight to the point ok so what happened on the 8th at the club Aces that night Mr. Harris? He replied nothing it was like any other night only a little crazier being it was right after the championship game. Everybody was out having a good time celebrating you feel me? Now around 11:00pm or a little after all hell broke loose I was in the back of the club v.i.p statue you dig James had left already. So I see and hear people yelling, running, screaming, so I ran outside because I thought a fight had broke out or something like that. So after I got through the crowd of people I see this kid laid out on the sidewalk so I yelled out call 911 because the shit excuse my language didn't look good at all he wasn't breathing or talking so people who were around started saying somebody ran this kid over. So I got everybody out of the parking lot and that's when I myself called 911 but they took so long to get there that's why it looks like I took so long. But once again I am sorry for what happened to that kid I am it's a damn shame. Mr. Parks replied how do you know he wasn't breathing? Mr. Harris replied well I didn't but he sure looked like he wasn't breathing he looked gone there was blood everywhere his eyes rolled back into his head it looked like he checked out man. Mr. Parks replied did you check his pulse at any time? Mr. Harris replied no I didn't want to touch him. Mr. Parks replied why not? Mr. Harris replied I don't know I guess I didn't want to get caught up you know what I mean? Mr. Parks replied no I don't understand caught up? What do you mean by that? Caught up? Mr. Harris replied if I touch him my prints are on him and I didn't want the police thinking that I had anything to do with it. Mr. Parks replied I see I see so he could have been alive still but you did want to get involved? What if you could of possibly helped this young man though? Mr. Harris replied no he was gone already. Mr. Parks replied do you think that Kayshawn is responsible for this young man's death? Mr. Harris replied absolutely not. Mr. Parks replied why is that?

Mr. Harris replied because me and Kayshawn go way back if he did I'd know, plus Kayshawn wouldn't do something like that. Mr. Parks replied but accidents do happen don't they? Mr. Harris replied but I'd know trust me I'd know. Mr. Parks replied no further questions your honor. I said to myself do you believe this shit? He barely questioned him it was bullshit and this went on for months. This trial took forever it felt like all the press and media surrounding it I was drained. I had death threats you name it but no matter what interview after interview I beat them with the facts that first there was no video surveillance the night of the incident why? Two the manager is to James and three he bleeds just like us fuck him being famous take that away and he is one of us. As long as I kept beating them with this I felt I'd maintain the upper hand. But Sabastion and Christian felt that I was getting my ass kicked and needed to get to Mrs. Clark fast before the jury just lets James walk free. See it's never what you know it's what you can prove and without that video I couldn't prove shit. So I decided to pay Mrs. Clark a visit at her residence. When I got there I knocked at the door and she yelled who is it? I replied it is me Attorney Jacob Cass. Mrs. Clark then opened the door slightly to see if it were really me. Once she saw that it was me she placed the baseball bat down that she had in her hand and let me in. once I was inside I could see that she was very scared as if the baseball bat didn't already give that away though. I said to her Ms. Clark I know that you are very nervous and that this is a lot on you but look if you really saw what you say you saw I'm going to need that video. I thought that I wouldn't need it but I do I am getting my ass handed to me in that courtroom lets end this once and for all what do you say? We all want to go home? Ms. Clark replied then what huh? You're getting death threats Cass so am I. I am fucking scared for my life and you can't protect me you can barely protect you. So I ask you what can you do for me? I give you that video and I am a dead women and you know that Cass. I replied ok look if you give me the video I will put you in police custody. Mrs. Clark replied fuck that I don't trust the police. I replied ok what about witness protection? You get a new name a new identity all that what do you say? Mrs. Clark replied I want a plane ticket out of here and a lot of money and the video is yours. I replied so you're not interested in witness protection? Mrs. Clark replied plus that witness protection shit too but my location and the money. I replied done ok how much do you want? Mrs. Clark replied 20 thousand dollars and a ticket to Aspen. I replied I don't know if I can make that happen I mean 20 thousand dollars and a ticket to Aspen that's a lot Mrs. Clark work with me here. Mrs. Clark replied first class ticket and that's my final offer Cass and I want to be gone before the verdict or the video is shown in court deal or no deal take it or leave it Cass? I exhaled and replied fuck man I don't know if I can make that happen but Mrs. Clark at least let me view the video before I ask to make sure that it is authentic? Mrs. Clark replied come on Cass you can get it they will give it to you because I got the hit and run on tape I video taped the whole damn thing on my cell phone. This video will destroy James career and put him behind bars give me what I want and it's yours or I sell it to the press but either way I am gone. I replied ok ok no don't do that let me talk to my boss and I will see what I can do but for now can you let me view it please? Mrs. Clark said sure here it is. I said to myself "oh my god" man she was right she played it for me and it was the whole trial wrapped up as a big gift for me. I said to myself holy shit this is what I need oh my god the whole fucking thing right here. I told Mrs. Clark look I will be right back if not give me a day or two ok? Mrs. Clark replied I like you Cass mad people want this tape and my dumb ass is going to hold it for you do you know why? I replied no why? Mrs. Clark replied because you care about what you're doing. You're not just a suit your one of us you been through this shit before so I am going to wait you got 2 days get me my money and my ticket and it's yours. I replied oh yeah there is just one more thing though. Mrs. Clark replied yeah what's that? I replied you don't really have a husband do you? Mrs. Clark replied I do we just are not together anymore why do you ask? I replied no I just didn't see him and when you talk about leaving you just speak about you leaving not the both of you that's all. I replied anyways thank you Mrs. Clark I am on it I will make it happen I will try my absolute best. Then I left and went straight to the office to speak with Sabastion and tell him everything that is going on and get this money but the question is will he go for it? Id stop at nothing to get him to say yes. So when I got to the office after speeding down the highway I went straight to my office to go over what I was going to tell Sabastion. How the fuck do I ask him for that type of money man? I took the fucking case for free then I'm going to ask for 20 thousand dollars that's what I'm going to hear. I'm going to get shitted on but that tape is the whole case and I needed it bad. So once I was ready I got up walked out my office and into Sabastion's and said Sabastion look i was just at Mrs. Clarks residence and she has the whole hit and run recorded on tape or rather her cell phone. I can end this trial right now with this video. Sabastion replied Jacob there is a price for everything I think you know that. So how much does Mrs. Clark want for this video? And how do you know that it is real? I replied well first off it's real because it's straight from her own cell phone and you see it all it is James sir. And money yes she wants of course and a lot of it plus protection. Sabastion replied protection? And how much Cass? I replied well she is scared for her life she wants a first class ticket to Aspen from there she wants to enter into the witness protection program. Sabastion replied I'm sure we could arrange that but how much money is she asking for Jacob? I replied she wants 20 thousand dollars to start a new life but Sabastion I need this video hell we need this video it is the whole case in a gift wrapped for us what do you say? Sabastion replied twenty thousand dollars is a lot of money shit but you are right this video is the case and we can't afford her to sell it to the press. Sabastion continues my only other concern is why didn't she do that already? I replied I have no idea maybe they didn't offer enough? Or maybe she really cares? I don't know all I do know is that we need it and we are wasting a lot of valuable time here don't you think? Sabastion replied yes perhaps you are right, look I don't have it now but I will get you the money by tomorrow and great work Jacob just make sure you bring this home for us. I replied oh I will now with this bet that. So the next day that morning bright and early I was up feeling great I couldn't sleep all night. So I decided to give my mother a call since it had been so long that we had spoken to one another. She told me that she had understood how busy that I must be but that she had missed me so much. And that she had been following the trial on television. Also that I am doing a great job. And everyone back home was so proud of me. That she tells all her friends about me. But of course there was the haters the people who want me dead or hate me for not praising their god instead felt like I was trying to crucify him. Nevertheless it was good hearing from her she told me that her health was good and that nothing much had changed except the money id been sending her monthly just to show her how much I love her. Well that morning around 8am I drove over to the office and met Sabastion around back. I jumped into his car and we headed over to the bank to get the money. Man by the time Sabastion handed me this heavy briefcase with the 20 thousand I said to myself "damn" this shit is really about to happen, I am about to win the trial of the decade. This was going to be huge the jury is going to be blow away the world will be too I don't think you all realize just how big this thing is really. So after I got the money I went straight to Mrs. Clark's place and handed the brief case to her. Mrs. Clark replied "wow" that was fast Cass very fast. I replied well my boss to my surprise went for it. Look this trial has drained us all and we want it to be over with as soon as possible. Mrs. Clark then handed over her cell phone and told me to keep it she will buy another one. Then she said so my ticket to Aspen? I replied oh well I'm going back to my office we can get one off of my computer then I will personally drive you to the airport myself ok? Deal? Mrs. Clark replied deal let me pack up my stuff give me a minute. I replied sure thing. I didn't like her neighborhood it was very ghetto, very hood, the place looked rough like it was falling apart the whole area made me very nervous. I drove a very nice company Mercedes-Benz and I didn't like how people looked at me but I knew it wasn't me it was the love they had for the man I was about to bring down. So when Mrs. Clark was done I was more than happy to leave I drove so fast back to the office after throwing three heavy suitcases in my trunk. Once I got back to the office Mrs. Clark and I were greeted by Sebastion and he asked to view the video in fact so did Christian and the entire office. Everyone upon viewing it said "well congratulations Cass you did it" tomorrow you will be the man. They believe that I had this case won as soon as I show the footage of the incident. So I got Mrs. Clark her one way first class ticket to Aspen leaving from Los Angeles California and she was so happy and very nervous at the same time. Now by the time that it was time to get Mrs. Clark to LAX for her flight I asked her so what are your plans? I mean you have twenty grand and your headed to Aspen why Aspen? I never asked? And what are your plans once you get there? Mrs. Clark replied I don't know Aspen I hear is beautiful and nobody will find me there. And what will I do? I don't know maybe become a fashion designer what do you think Cass? I replied you can do whatever you set your mind to my dear. Before exiting the car upon arriving at the airport Mrs. Clark asked me to stay in touch with her to make sure she is safe can I do that? I replied yes I will after you are placed into witness protection and you are settled in I will contact you if possible ok. Mrs. Clark replied ok thank you Mr. Cass thank you for everything. I replied no Mrs. Clark I really thank you for all your help. Mrs. Clark replied don't forget about me when you are a big star and have a hot girlfriend laughing. I replied never now go on before you are late take care of yourself and be safe. Mrs. Clark replied I will and she was gone. That next morning at 10:00am was court and I was about to drop a bombshell on the jury that would change the whole course of this trial for good. Man I had on my best suit and all it had belonged to my father so it meant a lot to me. And then all you heard was please "Please rise for the honorable Jude Nelson" as the courtroom rises. Then the judge entered the room and said you may all be seated, so I hear Attorney Cass that you have some evidence that you wish to submit to the court this morning? I replied I do your honor. Judge Nelson replied and has it been reviewed yet Cass? I replied yes your honor it has. Judge Nelson replied good you may be seated Cass. As Judge Nelson continued to say Good Morning to the court now let us proceed Attorney Cass. Now when it was my turn to deliver my closing argument it went a little something like this. Good Morning ladies and gentleman of the jury, you know a lot has been said about me throughout the course of this trial things like he is to young, he is to inexperienced, his heart is in the right place but, this trial hits to close to home for him. And I say your right am I young? Yes to young? no, am I inexperienced? Inexperienced as in is this my first actual case? Yes but am I qualified? Yes I wouldn't be here if I weren't. I've worked on a ten of cases but this is my actual first one. And last but not least does this trial hit close to home for me? Ladies and gentleman of the jury my father the late great Jacob Cass Sr was killed by a hit and run driver. This man walked and my father is in a casket so does this trial hit close to home for me? Yes it very much does. Am I impartial to reasoning because it hits so close to home? No. I was appointed to counsel because I am the best man for the job because it hits so close to home.

Ladies and gentleman I stand here before you today because it hits that close to home I stand for justice, I fight for justice, I fight for you. I fight for you all so much I took this case for free not a dime and not to crucify Kayshawn James but rather to stop injustice like what happened to my father happen to anybody. That is why I am here today that is why I decided to practice law. This trial to me wasn't ever about Kayshawn James, this trial wasn't about my father, this trial wasn't about money, this trail was about justice. Like I've said before ladies and gentleman I actually am a huge fan of Kayshawn James like we have heard throughout this whole trial he is great, he won the title and put Los Angeles on the map he truly is a great athlete and maybe this all was a mistake an accident but a kid lost his life a mother and father lost a son so superstar or not someone has to pay for that people. So I ask that you please open your minds and your hearts and bring the Johnson family closure we can't bring Brandon back but we can bring him justice the power is in your hands people. Now with that being said I'd like to ask to the stand Mr. Doug Harris. Mr. Harris takes the stand and I say Good Morning Mr. Harris. He replied Good Morning Sir. I replied now Mr. Harris I remind you that you are still under oath do you swear to tell the truth and the whole truth so help you god? Mr. Harris replied again I do. I replied good now I have here a video that I promised you that I would obtain as the jury gasps in disbelief as cameras begin to flash the judge yells "order in the court". I continued now Mr. Harris for your sake I'm going to show you this video before I show the court so that maybe you can help me figure this whole thing out ok? Mr. Harris replied ok sure. I replied good I approach the bench and press play on the video as Mr. Harris watches it. His face turning white in disbelief or from being scared. After the video is over I than ask can you describe or rather tell me who the man is outside the truck? Mr. Harris replied no not really. I replied no not really? Do you need me to put it up on the big screen then for you? Mr. Harris replied no you don't need to. Ok so under oath yet again Mr. Harris I ask you who is this man standing outside of the truck? Mr. Harris replied "ok ok it's me" as the jury and courtroom gasps. I replied ok so you weren't in the back of the club vip status when the incident took place you were outside in the parking lot right? Mr. Harris replied yes. I replied ok so Mr. Harris you lied in the court of law that is punishable up to 10 years prison time so I ask you to come clean. Again now who car is that in the video? Better yet who is the driver that you are talking to in the video? Mr. Harris replied I ain't doing that big dog I ain't doing that. I replied doing what Mr. Harris? I don't understand? Mr. Harris replied where we come from it's all about loyalty dog and I'm not going out like that so fuck you Cass Straight like that fuck you Kayshawn is a good dude I'm out. As Mr. Harris sits up and walks off of the witness stand he yells "L.A. Shooters baby all day everyday yo" "Champions" "King James" ya'll know "Loyalty" "death before dishonor" we live by that code nigga. The judge screams "order" as the bailiff takes Mr. Harris away cameras flashing and it is now pandemonium in the courtroom. The judge yelling "order in the court" Harris is yelling all while James has his head down because he knows his faith is almost sealed, Harris outburst clearly showed his guilt for James. Now after the courtroom settled down there was nothing left to do but to show the jury the video and put the nail in the coffin. I then asked the judge for permission to show the video to the jury and I was granted the permission to do so. The video clearly showed that Mrs. Clark had recorded Kayshawn James leaving the club drunk stumbling to his truck and sitting right in the driver's seat as he spoke to Mr. Harris from outside of the truck. Then he proceeds to back out his parking spot drive fast through the parking lot and slamming right into Brandon Johnson. Then Mr. Harris runs over to the truck checks on Kayshawn before even checking on the young man first after he appears to be dead already Mr. Harris tells Mr. James to leave the seen and he will take care of it for Kayshawn to go. The jury and the courtroom was stunned and in complete silence as I looked over to my left to see the expression on Kayshawn's face. He was in tears I looked over to my right and saw the Johnson family also in tears as I then stopped the video and said "the defense rests it's case your honor." The judge replied court is hereby agerned for the day we will all be back here tomorrow morning at 10:00am for deliberation court is dismissed. I then went and shook both Mr. and Mrs. Johnson's hands as they both gave me a hug and said "Thank you Mr. Cass for all your help." I replied it my pleasure I will see you both tomorrow morning as I then left the courtroom to be greeted by Sebastion outside the doors and into a sea of news reporters to answer a few questions. As reporters yell "Attorney Cass" "Mr. Cass" "How does it feel to take down Kayshawn James?" "You are a star now how does it feel?" I replied I feels great to be able to serve justice but it's not over yet the jury hasn't made a verdict yet. As a reporters yells "oh now your just being cocky Cass you got this and you know it." I replied it could still go anyway. A reporter then asked "if James is convicted what will he be facing?" I replied I don't have the answers to that question just yet let's just wait and see. As I rush through the crowd to get to the car I say "ok thank you all for the questions I have to go now see you all tomorrow morning. "wait Mr. Cass" "Mr. Cass" as I jumped in to the car and speed off. In the car Sebastion looks over at me smiling and says "wow" Jacob i am so proud of you, your father is smiling down on you right now your first case and you are about to win the biggest case in history. i replied i told you all along to let me take this one that everything was going to be alright didn't I tell you that? Sebastion replied but what if the jury doesn't convict him then what? I replied with what they just saw how could they not? Not only was it a hit and run but now it was also a cover up he is finished he only better hope that god and the judge have mercy on him because i sure as hell don't. The next morning I had on my best suit on and got to court humbled, nervous, and excited. Now all rise for the honorable Judge Nelson Burke He replied you may be seated. The judge says are we ready for deliberations? The foreman replied yes your honor we are. Judge replied ok i am going to ask that the jury be retired to the deliberation room at this time to consider a verdict we will reases until then court is now dismissed. Now i drove straight back to the office and just waited just like the rest of the world was doing. I was sure that there was no other way that the jury could find him to be innocent not with what they just saw there was just no way. So i told Sebastion that Kayshawn James was no murderer but he will go down just not for murder. I told Kayshawn's lawyer we are not going after him for murder although that is what the media wanted to say but nevertheless he is guilty just not of murder. This is why i stress that accidence do happen but regaurdless someone needs to pay for this young mans death. Yes he was young what was he doing out that late anyways they stress? Teen or not those are all legitimate questions but the fact still remains that he hit and killed this young man accident or not and left the sense of the crime and he must pay for his accident. So as Sebastion and I sat in the office waiting after about 3 hours or so went by we got the call that the jury has reached a verdict. We were in disbeleif that they had taken so long to reach a verdict and were very concerned for a victory because of it but the time had come the time that the whole world had been waiting for had come. Sebastion and I rushed to the courthouse through traffic and the mob sense that awited us in and outside of the courthouse. All rise for the honorable Judge Nelson Burke, you may be seated. The judge replied ok so the jury has reached a verdict please bring the jury back in. As the jury beings to walk back into the courtroom with nervousness. The foreman passes the verdict to the balif who then passes it to Judge Burke and upon reading the verdict he then allows the verdict to be read out loud to the court. And here it goes the moment of truth will Kayshawn Michael James please rise for sentencing as he stood tall above the courtroom. We the people find the defendent Kayshawn Michael James Guilty of first degree vehicular manslaughter and negligent homicide hit and run. As the courtroom goes crazy as camaras begin to flash Kayshawn sits back down and puts his head down as he cries and says to himself "oh my god what have i done to deserve this punishment? The judge yells "order in the court" "order in the court" as everyone begins to calm down the judge says please rise Mr. James as Kayshawn stands back up the judege says you are hear by sentenced to 3 to 15 years in Pelican Bay State Prison and I would like to say to you Mr. James that you are one hell of an athlete but leaving that young man there to die was horrible. With that being said the jury is now dismissed and thank you all for your civil duties as they are greatly appricated. And that was it i was now offically the biggest attorney in the nation the entire world just watched this entire case unfold right before their very eyes. When i left the courtroom i gave Mr. and Mrs. Johnson a big hug and told them "thank you for allowing me to avenge your sons death and at the sometime allow myself some closure for my father as well." Mr. Johnson replied No thank you Mr. Cass i have never seen anyone quite as determine as you are, How much do we owe you? I replied like i said months ago you owe me nothing take care Mr. Jonson and if you ever need me for anything don't hesitate to call you have my number, oh and also if anybody needs any attorney refer them my way that is all i ask. Mr. Johnson replied i will Mr. Cass you have my word on that thank you again. Now when i left the courtroom it was hell getting out, outside there where news reporters, fans of Kayshawn that hated my guts, and fans now of my own but nevertheless for the first time in my life i could honestly admitt that for the first time in my life i felt like the man. Like I had done something so good but yet people hated me for being the man behind putting Kayshawn away the paper was calling me "The man behind the madness". And of course leaving the courtroom i have to speak to the press so here i am Sebastion and I standing side by side on the steps outside of the courtroom and someone from the press asks "Attorney Cass" you are all in the press, all over every magazine, your huge, how does it feel winning the biggest case in history and of your career possibly and it's only your first case? I replied it feels good to have won and helped the Johnson Family. You see i'm from a small town in Washington so i can do without the media, the press, the magazines, the hype, all that I am just a regular attorney just like the rest I fight for what I believe in. And like i've said throughtout this case it was hard to have to put are favorite athlete behind bars but it had to be done i wish nothing but the best for the Johnson and James families it is rough on us all. Then from out the crowd someone yells "Die Cass" "Rot in hell" I replied Do you hear that? You see it is a gift and a curse. One more question then i have to go. Mr. Cass my question is what's next for Attorney Jacob Cass? I replied "wow" you know what that is actually a very good question oddly enough. Well I guess I need to actually move in my place i'm sure my roommate would like me out laughing umm I guess I just want to continue to win cases and help others out who could use a good genuwine, caring, lawyer. And with that being said Almonds and Almonds is at your service thank you ladies and gentleman but I really have to go so have a wonderful, safe, and Blessed day drive home safe take care and I left straight back to the office Sebastion and I. When i got back to the office I literally walked into a standing ovation everybody was so happy and proud except for one person who I could tell wasn't all that happy and of course that had to be Christian. With everyone clapping and celebrating their was cookie, cake, champiagne, you name it. Not only was I the most successful attorney in the nation but I single handly put Almonds and Almonds on the map as the most popular law firm in the country. Christian approached me and said "Good Job Superstar" Mrs. Clark really came through and saved the day for you and this firm good work. Almost if saying that I didn't do a good job that she did. So I simply laughed it off and replied yeah i did do a good job like I told you all that I would. He chuckled and said that you did. So after everybody gave me hugs and said what they had to say I left back home or rather to Blakes I was so exhausted but on the way home I called my mother who was so happy for me she said that i was the home town hero they were calling me the "Avenger of Aberdeen" and my mother couldn't be anymore happier for me she knew who I was and how much this ment to me. She told me that not only was she proud of me but that my father would have been too. She told me that I was all over the television and newspapers that all over Aberdeen no matter where she goes people would treat her differently and that she didn't like all the attention though. I told her not to worry about it that it would all die down eventually. She asked me when I was coming back home to visit her? I told her soon very soon as the attention over here was even worse. She told me that she didn't want to move to L.A. that she wanted to stay in Aberdeen and that I should move back because she didn't like me being in L.A. she always feared something bad would happen to me out here now even more so now with the fame that I had recently obtained she was very paranoid much like my father was. You see I could deal with Aberdeen I grew up there but Los Angeles was an entirly different place with different rules. Los Angeles demanded your popularity Aberdeen praised you for it. After speaking to my mother on the drive home I finally got into the front door of Blakes place as he had music blasting it was like walking into a party or something like that. Blake runs up to me shakes my hand and says "bro you are the man now" you did it Jacob we have to go out and party tonight we have to celebrate bro. I replied by the looks of this place you have already started Blake this place is a total mess what's going on? Blake replied Jacob you are the top attorney in the country do you know how many dorme parties UCLA students are throwing in your honor? You know how many clubs are going to be happenening tonight? Yeah certain clubs hate you but nevermind those we are going to hit up the ones that love you and have your back. A couple of friends where over hanging out waiting on you man Jacob I had blow, women, you name it we have to celebrate bro what do you say? I replied bro that is cool and all but if it's all the same with you i'm exhausted I think i'm just going to take a nap do you mind turning down the music a bit so I can get some rest please? Blake replied rest? nap? with this confused look on his face he replied man that is so typical of you Jacob you are the top attorney in the country you are a workaholic all you do is work. But you have worked all them days, all them hours, you worked your ass off through college, law School, all that to become the man and I couldn't be anymore proud of you but god damn it Jacob you need a real life outside of work i've been telling you this for years now. Look Jacob how many girlfriends have you had? I replied I don't want to do this right now Blake. Blake replied no Jacob seriously how many? I replied I don't know what difference does it make? Blake replied well you do like pussy right? I replied of course I do i'm not gay if that's what your asking. Blake replied ok good all i'm saying is that you have to live bro all I ever do is see you work you never have fun so tonight i'm taking you out it's on me your going to drink, get fucked up, fuck bitches, and party hard, because you deserve it what do you say bro? I replied I have to go pay this realitor for my place. Blake replied I tell you what take your nap when you wake go handle that then tonight we party what do you say? I said to myself maybe he is right shit I can't remember my last relationship it's been that long. It probably was a girl named Hazel my freshman year of high school I lost my virgenity to and haven't been with anyone since. I took that break up pretty hard and focused more on work but come to think about it that is why she left me in the first place I guess i've always been a workaholic. So I said to myself look i'm young, i'm goodlooking, i'm successful, I might as well go out and have a good time right? I told Blake ok sure tonight your on lets do it. Blake replied "Hell yeah" that is what i'm talking about let's celebrate ok cool let me let the superstar sleep i'll wake you up in a few hours what time do you need to meet the realitor at? I replied at 4:00pm. Blake replied ok it's 1:30pm now i'll wake you at 3:00 or 3:30 ok? I replied ok thanks. Blake replied "no problem" it takes you to become famous to come out the house and chill ain't this a bitch as he laughs and walks out the apartment and closes the door. When he came back and woke me up at 3:00pm I got up and drove over to meet the realitor and give him the deposit on the house. I was so happy I looked around and said to myself "wow" this is mine all mine my first house a place of my own my career is at an all time high it seemed as if I was sitting on top of the world. The deposit alone was enough so all I was able to put in the place was a couch I think I spent so much time on Blakes couch that now I think I like sleeping on couches rather than a bed. A nyway back to Blakes I went to pretty much go back to bed I was so tired I could barely keep my eyes open. When I got back to Blakes he was already passed out in his room and so I did the same turned off the pagers and phones and passed out right there on the couch. He then woke up around 9:00pm because the radio from in his room was blaring which in turn then woke me up. Blake then says "wake up" superstar it is time to hit the club bro get dressed and lets do this. I replied "i'm up, i'm up" I then go take a shower to freshen up and to wake myself up. I then asked Blake what suit should I wear? Blake replied Jacob tonight we are not attorneys or med students we are regular guys going out to a club to chill no suits tonight you aren't Jacob Cass the attorney tonight you are regular Jacob Cass the person my friend, my brother, can you handle that? I replied but you said we are celebrating the win as an attorney so i'm alittle confused? Blake replied Jacob wear a dress shirt a pair of jeans and some sneakers that will work bro. I replied ok sounds good and got dressed so by the time I was ready to go so was Blake. So here we are around 10:00pm and we are headed to Los Angeles best hip hop club called "The Room" this place was packed when we arrived there were so many people there and I was treated like a celebrity right through the door anything I wanted I could have. Blake and I had our own private booth and all the DJ even gave me a shout out all courtesy of Blake how he had all these connections I didn't know until later on in the night. I wasn't use to all this attention Blake kept bringing drinks after drinks Champainge all night Ace of spades you name it we had it. But throughout the entire night I could only see and focus on this one particular woman because she didn't take her eyes off of me all night long. She was beautiful and way out of my league but shit we had so many drinks and I stupidly enough told Blake about this female and what does he do? He replied who that chick over at the bar? I replied yes she is hot and she has been looking at me. Blake yells "waiter" here is a big tip you see that woman at the bar with the red dress on? The waiter replied yes I do. Blake replied tell her this drink is on my brother Jacob Cass the motherfucking man and tell her that when she is finished to come over to our table ok? The waiter replied ok will do sir can I get you anymore drinks? Blake replied yes you can and keep them coming we are celebrating baby!!!!! So as we continue to party hard Blake now is bringing all these woman to our booth and they are all talking to me and what not but it was like I was drown to this woman at the bar who mind you never came over after the drink instead drank it and sent one back over saying "Thank you that was sweet" written on a napkin delivered by the waitress. After a while I then said fuck it I already had a good buzz going so I walked over to her and introducded myself like the gentleman I was. I said Hi my name is Jacob. She replied Hi my name is Elizabeth my friends call me Liz for short. I replied beautiful name may I call you Liz? Elizabeth replied well that all depends. I replied on what? she replied are you trying to be my friend? with her seductive voice and gorgoeus eyes I replied yes I want to be your friend. Elizabeth replied ok then asked well are you going to sit down Jacob? I replied yes of course i'm sorry as I was hyptnotized by her beauty. She then asked so what brings you out tonight Jacob? I replied wait you don't know who I am? Elizabeth replied no am I suppose to? I replied no i'm sorry I just.....I don't know why I assumed you knew who I was that was rude of me i'm sorry about that. While Elizabeth begins to laugh I replied i'm sorry did I say something funny or something confused? Elizabeth replied yes I know who you are laughing you're Jacob Cass top shot attorney yes I do have and watch television although you are much more handsome on television as we both start laughing. I replied ha ha ha ok you got me. Elizabeth replied gosh relax are you always this transparent? Then says so let me guess your out here celebrating your victory right? I replied yes my friend dragged me out here tonight. Elizabeth replied well are you having fun Jacob? I replied I am now looking into her beautiful eyes I just wanted to kiss her I was so turned on by this woman it was unbelieveable. Then Elizabeth replied well since we are friends now what does a girl have to do to get a drink around here? let's turn up. I replied "Oh yeah right" I know how to tear up hey bartender? Bartender replied "yes Mr. Cass?" I replied get this beautiful woman whatever she wants what is your drink of choice? Elizabeth replied laughing turn up. I replied what is that? She replied laughing you said tear up it's turn up. I replied I knew that laughing come on what we drinking on Liz? Liz replied how about "Sex on the beach". I replied sex on the beach it is waiter keep them coming all night. The waiter replied yes sir. I asked so tell me about yourself Liz you know my name and what i'm doing here tonight so why are you out here tonight? Liz replied well i'm a hair dresser from Miami and I just moved out to L.A. for more money and better opportunity and well here I am and tonight I just want to have fun and get fucked up. I replied sounds fair enough so are you here with anybody tonight? Liz replied do you see that hot girl over there in that booth with that guy? I replied yes I do. Liz replied that is my friend Samantha she is the head bartender here and tonight is her night to train this girl behind the bar she is trying to get me a part-time job here. She is a friend and somewhat of a roommate she lives down the hall from me but she is always at my apartment she isn't doing such a good training job tonight either laughing. I told her don't leave me alone if I come out tonight but she did and found herself a man so I sat here alone. I replied yeah well my friend kind of did the same to me too. Liz replied so this is kind of like faith then huh? I replied I guess so. I then asked so what is your last name if you don't mind me asking? Liz replied it's West why am i in trouble Attorney Cass? I replied no I was just curious that's all. Liz replied well you know what curiousity did right? I replied no what? Liz replied it killed the cat. I replied very true. Liz replied well cheers to new friends and new beginings. And we knocked back drink after drink then Blakes comes over to the bar and says "Hey Jacob are you going to introduce me to your neww friend? I replied yes Blake this is Elizabeth, Liz this is my good friend and brother and ex roommate Blake. They both say hello to one another as Blake has to be all extra and kiss her hand and tell her how beautiful she is. Then the drinks keep coming as we were asked to join Blake back at the booth and as the night started to slow down the hard stuff began to come out and surprisingly it wasn't even from Blake it came from Liz. Liz asked if I wanted to do some cocaine just a few rails? I told her that I had never done it before. She told me that just alittle should be fine and as I was about to pass on the offer

Blake said if Jacob don't want to I will with you Liz I won't leave you hanging. Now at this point because of the whole drug thing going on I felt Blake was drawing her interest more than I was so I decided to do a few lines with them. Now here we are high off of cocaine and drunk off of alcohol and all I could think about was how good it would feel to be inside of Liz. I wanted this woman so fucking bad but I was so nervous to kiss her but after a few more bumps and a few more shots Liz leans over and say are you ever going to kiss me Jacob Cass? And right then and there I grabbed her face and shoved my tongue so far down her throat kissing her so passionatly that I could smell the moisture of her vagina. I felt like the man I had the hottest girl in the club by far plus everyone is treating me like a god for the win from the waiters and waitresses, to the bartenders, to the guest, all the way down to the Dj's in the house this night couldn't possibly get any better. Now Blake, his lady friend, myself, and my new friend Liz are all on the dance floor high as a kite but I was actually feeling good although I think we may have over done ourselves a bit but the night was slowing down and as Liz and I made out on the dance floor she wispered in my ear "do you want to get out of here?" Maybe go back to my place or something like that? I replied yeah i'd love to let's do that. Liz replied ok cool let's go "oh do you have a car here?" I replied yes I actually drove here with Blake how about yourself? Liz replied well I don't drive my girlfriend drove I just have to let her know that I am leaving ok? I replied ok yeah I better do the same let me tell Blake. So I told Blake that I was leaving the club with Liz and that we were going back to her place. He replied good for you bro that is what i'm talking about go nail that bitch to the wall. I replied yeah ok your messed up are you going to catch a ride with your friend? Blake replied of course I have to seal the deal my friend and I want to hear all about your night tomorrow to ok buddy? I replied ok will do be safe Blake I mean it. Blake replied always you too bro. And that was that off Liz and I go making our way out the club as everyone is taking my picture yelling "You the man Cass" as we exited to the car I asked ok where to Liz? She replied to my apartment which is not to far from here. She goes on to say don't make fun of me i'm still new out here and all I have in my place is a bed, a couch, and a television. I replied laughing you have me beat I just have a couch at my place I am a new home owner myself so I feel your pain on that one. So we drove over to Liz apartment and the whole car ride there she is taking bumps of cocaine and feeding me some as well. By the time we got to her place I felt like I was floating on clouds her place had white walls and was completely empty. We stood on her balcony while we drank, sniffed, and spoke and then she started doing some harder stuff I think it was acid I told her to ease up a bit but she told me that she is just trying to have a good time. Then we headed to the bedroom I was nervous as fuck but boy was I ever ready she then looks at me with that sexy seductive look on her face and asked me "Jacob do you want me?" I replied more than anything right now. Liz replied take my dress off. I replied ok and I slowly removed each shoulder strap one by one and un-zippered the back until her dress fell to the floor. Then Liz replied take off my bra. I replied ok then removed her bra her breast were amazing. Liz then replied kiss me all over and take off my thong. I then slowly started to kiss on her neck all the way down to her breast sucking on both nipples nibbling gently not to hard going lower down to her belly botton while I slowly removed her thong she had the body of a goddess she smelled and tasted so good. I then pushed her on the bed while I removed my shirt then pants then underwear my dick was so hard and I was so ready. I began to go down on her as she moans louder and louder in complete extacy when she had enough and couldn't take it anymore while her eyes rolled back into her head I slide inside of her deep wet pussy. She felt so good as her juices flowed and she wrapped around me like a glove I couldn't keep going slow anymore so I turned her around and began thrusting harder and harder as she tells me to pull her hair and slap her ass as I stroke in and out she can't take it anymore as she moans and yells with pleasure. Now her face is deep in the pillow as i'm stroking away I notice that the moans go away and so does the yelling I ask baby how does it feel? I'm about to cum baby but Liz didn't say anything back but at this point I couldn't stop as I climaxed all inside of her. I said to her baby that felt amazing oh my god Liz are you ok? As her head is still in the pillow as she lays motionless I turn her over and ask "Liz are you ok?" talk to me Liz? I said to myself oh my god Liz wake up are you ok? She wouldn't move for nothing. I checked her pulse and she didn't have one i said to myself Liz what the fuck please wake up. I began to perform CPR but nothing no luck I said to myself "oh my god she is dead" what the fuck? what the fuck am I suppose to do? I fucking can't call the cops they will pin this shit on me. I am a hated attorney this bitch has been drinking and smoking and snorting all night they will pin this all on me I can't call the cops the media would have a feild day with this they would love to curcify me shit what the fuck should I do? I kept asking myself yo my whole career everything I worked so hard for will be destroyed what the fuck should I do? I knew if I called 911 that i would be the main suspect I know how this shit works they would pin this shit on me. So being drunk and coked out my mind I got dressed and got the fuck up out of there as fast as I could I didn't know what else to do so I panic and left. I drove straight to Blakes and he wasn't there I tried calling him and no answer I called Sebastion and samething no answer it was like 3:30am. So I drove back to my place and paced up and down up and down like what am I going to do? The police will be over this soon as Liz girlfriend goes to check on her and either way you look at it i'm fucked. All this is Blakes fault "go out Jacob" "go get pussy Jacob" you see why I stay to myself? This is fucking bullshit what did I get myself into? I couldn't even sleep I sat up all night long and around 8:00am that next morning Sebastion called me asking how did the club go? I replied not good at all look Sebastion i'm in a lot of trouble. Sebastion replied Jacob what happen? I replied I met this girl at the club last night we hit it off and well anyways we went back to her place we had unprotected sex and the bitch died while we were having sex. Sebastion replied laughing stop playing Jacob. I replied i'm not playing would I make some shit up like this? Sebastion replied how do you know that she is dead? maybe she just passed out. I replied no she is dead Sebastion she wasn't breathing at all. Sebastion replied how much did you both drink? I replied she drank a lot I mean we both did plus there was cocaine involved and she did acid too. Sabastion replied she probably died of an overdose your good Jacob just try to get some rest ok. I replied maybe your right but I feel bad leaving her there and not calling 911 but you know they will pin it on me. Sebastion replied it's going to come back to you anyways when they find your semen inside of her. I replied but I have no police record and would like to keep it that way I need your help. Sebastion replied ok well if people say they saw you all together they will question you and when that time comes you need to just cooporate and tell them what happened. I replied ok I will thanks Sebastion. Sebastion replied next time wear a condom superstar now get some rest. I replied ok I will. Well it didn't take long for shit to hit the fan because later that day Liz friend came by to see her and had a key to the apartment and let herself in and found Liz dead body laying in the bed neighbors heard screams as her friend dials 911. 911 emergercy operator what is your emergency? Crying yes my name is Samantha Collins my friend Elizabeth is not breathing I think she is dead. Operator replied what is your location mam? Samantha replied yes it is 15161 Traverse Lane. Operator replied ok i'm sending paramedics over now ok hang tight. Paramedics arrive and so does the good old L.A.P.D who really don't like me they are all fans of James and I put him away. Now the lead detective is a prick named Armstrong he was known for being crooked and a dick but who knows. Anyways my problems were about to get even worst because the next day bright and early I get a call from Sebastion telling me Armstrong is ruling Elizabeth West death as a homicide and guess who is the main suspect? You guessed it me. Samantha Collins tells Detective Armstrong that her friend Elizabeth was last seen with me that Elizabeth told her that we were coming to her apartment. Sebastion tells me Jacob it's even worst when I asked why do you say that? Sebastion replied because the crime sense has your DNA all over it Jacob your cum, your blood, she had your tie wrapped around her neck they found her body tied to the bed with her face buried in a pillow and her hands tied to the bed post. I replied no fucking way Sebastion I never did that. Sebastion replied there were letters between the two of you both all sorts of stuff implicating you as her murderer. I replied Sebastion somebody is setting me up. Sabastion replied needless to say Jacob this doesn't look good you need to turn yourself in before this gets even worst for you. I replied Sebastion I didn't kill that girl i'm being set up maybe by James people I don't know but I didn't kill that girl. You believe me don't you? Sebastion replied of course I do but Armstrong is going to be gunning for you. I replied fuck Armstrong I need to find out what's going on hold him off just give me a few days to clear my name and find out who set me up. Sebastion replied I will but hurry up Jacob. I replied I will. Now I had to really evaluate the situation but I was so confused as to who could or would have done this to me. I t only made sense to me that it was Kayshawn James people but it could be anybody a teammate, a friend, a family member, a fan, this was going to be tough so I decided to pay Mr. James a visit in the prison before this shit goes national. Now legally James doesn't have to speak to me at all but given his current situation I felt that I could purswey him into telling me something by bribing him or giving him false hope fuck it this is my life and career on the line and I was desparate. Now when I got to the jail everybody immediately gave me shit you see i'm the guy who put this man away to some people I ruined his career and now i'm visiting him? So needless to say I wasn't popular among the jails. So I sat down with Kayshawn and got striaght to the point with him by saying so what is this Kayshawn payback or something? You know for what it's worth I didn't want to have to lock you up you are probably my favorite athlete but Kayshawn I was doing my fucking job do you understand me? I didn't set you up or frame you I had proof and you know that. Kayshawn replied Mr. Cass what are you talking about? I repleid come on Kayshawn don't play dumb with me just tell me what you want to make this go away? Kayshawn replied what are you talking about Cass? pay back? I really have no idea what you are talking about? You come up in here accusing me of god knows what man look at where i'm at dog the place you put me at but I moved past that i'll get my shot again one day. I replied i'm talking about the girl Kayshawn her apartment please stop bullshitting me who did you have set me up? Kayshawn replied laughing yo I guess karma really is a bitch ain't it? But yo Cass I have no idea what your talking about yo what girl? what apartment? set you up? yo get up out of here Cass maybe it's somebody else life you destroyed be gone man get the fuck up out of here Cass. I replied look obviously this isn't about money but look if you help me I can help you ok? If not you maybe a friend, a family member, an obsessed fan, I don't know but if you help me find out who set me up maybe I can help you out in here what do you say? Kayshawn replied first off it wasn't me I have not a clue as to what you are talking about and no friend or family member of mine would do anything without talking to me first. Now I can't do anything about no fans you feel me? But what is it that you want me to do? And what can you do for me Cass? I replied well first off I can possibly get your time in here reduced. Kayshawn replied yeah and how can you do that? I replied i'm Jacob Cass I know a lot of people in high places you just let me worry about that. Kayshawn replied what do you want from me Cass? I replied find out who set me up, ask around the prison, friends, teammates, family, and i'll make sure your time is reduced by atleast half you got my word on that what do you say? Kayshawn replied your word don't mean shit to me but you must be in some deep shit so you gonna tell me what happened or what? I replied i met some lady in a club we went back to her place and next thing I know she is dead her entire apartment was set up and staged to look like I did it end of story you happy now? Kayshawn laughing wow and you suspect me and my people did this to you why? I replied for the obvious I put you in here plus I have no enemies except for anyone affiliated or associated with you. Kayshawn replied hmm I see so where did you meet this woman at? I replied at The Room, and then it downed on me that James really knew nothing and you might be asking yourself why? Good question if you were and it's simple it's becausse i'm a lawyer we know when someone is lying just like I knew in that courtroom. He was being very helpful and I could tell that he was being very honest. I replied you know of that club right? Kayshawn replied of course I do and if I where you id ask around there like you did about me at the Aces. He was right because this all started at The Room club with this woman Liz so I needed to go back there and see what I could find out go back to the beginning and start all over again. I replied yes you are right but on your end I need you to still ask teammates, family, friends, whatever you can ok? Kayshawn replied ok i'll see what I can do Cass. I replied thank you Kayshawn. He replied no problem I have nothing but time up in here anyways be safe Cass. I replied I will you too. And I left and headed striaght for the club The Room to see what I could dig up. But on my way to the club I get a call from Blake telling me that I need to get to his place that a Detective Armstrong is at the house looking for me to ask me a few questions. I told Blake to tell him that I would be there that I am on my way. Now when I pulled up to Blakes house I got out the car walked up to the door and as I turned the knob to open the door Blake swang it open and said you just missed him he wanted to ask you a few questions Jacob what is really going on bro? I replied I don't know someone is trying to frame me. Blake replied who is? I replied that is what I need to figure out. Blake replied bro this girl is dead they think you killed her Jacob. I replied that is bullshit. Jacob i'm sorry bro this is all my fault I shouldn't have made you go out and Celebrate. I replied look I don't need to hear all that right now, right now I need you to help me find out any and everything you can find out about an Elizabeth West ok? I need to find out who set me up and why. Blake replied ok I will but what are you going to do now? I replied i'm packing a few things and i'm going to stay at my place or a hotel until this thing blows over. Blake replied what about Armstrong? I replied fuck Armstrong if he asks i'm not here everytime ok? Blake replied ok well your not going to speak to him? I replied not face to face tell him to call me if he comes back here ok? Blake replied ok Jacob be safe bro aye take my car they won't notice you and it's in the back in case they see you leave. I replied ok thanks i'll return it in a few days here are the keys to mine and I walked out the back door to a loud gun cock and loud yells of "freeze Cass get down" and all I could think of was they won't shoot me there are way to many inocent people out here right now so my first gut instinct was just to simply run and that is what the fuck I did. So rather than to shoot me it became a foot chase I ran and ran as fast as I could and got the hell out of dodge with managing to flee the police I ran into a ditch and hid in a sewer for a couple of hours. So now did I not only have no car but I had no clothes as well all I could think about was did Blake set me up? I mean he did beg me to go to the club in the first place but then he tells me to use his car which was parked in the back and I walk right into the police I mean what the fuck was that? I was so fucking confused I didn't want to beleive that it was Blake but right now all evidence suggest and points to him like the crime sense points to me. I said to myself maybe he is mad that I won the case? or maybe he liked Elizabeth? I mean she was the hottest girl in the club. I don't know but when the coast was clear I left the sewer and went striaght to The Room club because to go back to Blakes it would be way to hot over there. I remembered that Liz told me that the bartender was her friend slash roomamte that was trying to get her a job there. She is also the one who called the cops and gave them my name so I needed to speak to her and find out what she knows about Blake, Liz, and even possibly Kayshawn James. I just needed to ask questions and get as much possible information as I can. When I got to The Room I saw Samantha at the bar and immediately walked up to it and said id like a shot of peach Ci-roc on the rocks please. As Samantha looks over and says i'm not suppose to be talking to you besides I don't talk to rapist or murderers either. I replied well lucky for you that im neither one so listen can I speak to you please? I just need to ask you a few questions please and then I will leave you never have to see me again? Samantha replied your lucky i'm going on break let's go sit at a table you have five minutes and then I call the cops. I replied come on Samantha i'm no killer i'm an attorney can we talk out back? Samantha replied what so you can rape and kill me to? I don't think so look i'm calling the cops. I replied no look wait wait don't call ok a table is fine. Samantha replied and how do you know my name? I replied Liz told me it. So we sit down and Samantha says ok what do you want to know? I replied first off do you know who I am? Samantha replied yes your Attorney Jacob Cass the attorney who put Kayshawn James behind bars your also the man who raped and killed my friend Liz. I replied I didn't rape and kill her we drank, we sniffed, we did it all drugs killed her not me. Samantha replied yet your here talking to me and she is in a pine box. I replied I don't know what happened all I know is that we had consensual sex she was a beautiful woman i'd never hert her. So how long did you know her for? Samantha replied about 3 weeks. I replied yes she mentioned that she was new to Los Angeles she was a hair dresser from Miami that she was out here looking for better opportunity. Do you know a guy named Blake at all? Samantha replied you mean the guy you were here with that night? I replied yes you know him? Samantha replied everybody knows him he is a regular in here. I replied oh ok did he and Liz no eachother before that night? Samantha replied no that was Liz first night here. I replied so was mine that is strange. Samantha replied yeah it is you know what else is weird? I replied what is that? Samantha replied the fact that she told you that she was a hair dresser from Miami.

I replied why is that weird? Samantha replied because she told me that she was a hair dresser to just not from Miami. I replied where did she tell you she was from Samantha? Samantha replied she told me some place in Washington i can't really remember though. My heart about dropped in my lap I replied Washington where in Washington try to remember? Samantha replied I don't know I don't remember if she told me that or not. I replied try to remember this is important did she? Samantha replied um I don't know why is that important? I replied because i'm from Washington. Samantha replied um maybe Arlean something like that I think. I replied Aberdeen? Samatha replied yeah that's it Aberdeen, Aberdeen Washington. My face turned pale in confustion. Samantha replied are you ok Mr. Cass you look like you just seen a ghost or something. I replied no i'm ok thank you for your time Samantha I no you have to get back to work listen you take care of yourself ok? Now in confustion and in frustration Samantha replied umm ok you sure you are ok? I replied i'm good take care and again thank you for your time. Samantha replied ok you too I guess. I said to myself really what the fuck is going on? This woman not only was her first night at that club just like mine but now she is from my home state and city too? this wasn't no fucking coincidence at all man. So I checked into a hotel by using cash only no credit or debit cards because by now my facc was all over the television again but this time saying "Star attorney Jacob Cass is now the main suspect in the murder of a young hair dresser from Miami" Police say Cass is wanted in connection in the murder and rape of Elizabeth West. West moved out to Los Angeles to further her career she was only 25 if you have any information on the where abouts of attorney Jacob Cass you are to call the L.A.P.D. immediately as he is considered to be armed and dangerous. I said to myself armed and dangerous are you fucking kidding me? I needed to get out of this hotel and get to my house its not safe here anymore. Now on Sebastion's end he was visited by Detective Armstrong. Armstrong tells Sebastion look you need to turn your guy in. Sebastion replys I have no idea where he is at have you tried his house? Armstrong replied yes he got away somehow it won't happen again through best beleive that. Then I get a call from Dectective Armstrong myself on my cell phone telling me that he knows i'm at Hollywood Hotel and that he is coming for me. I replied Armstrong I didn't do this I was set up. Armstrong replied come into the office and let's talk about it Jacob. I replied your not listening to me Armstrong listen your not arresting me for something that I didn't do give me a few days to clear my name and fine out who set me up. Armstrong replied if someone set you up Jacob that is my job to find that out not yours let the L.A.P.D. handle this. I replied yeah because your doing such a good job now your after the wrong man. Armstrong replied we follow the evidence Cass just like you do turn yourself in and make this easier on all of us. I replied look Armstrong i'll find you the person who set me up but i'm not turning myself in because I didn't do this you can thank me later and I hung up on him. With a baseball hat and some sunglasses on that I had paid someone in the hotel for I got out again only this time I had to punch out a fellow police officer who recognized me when he yelled it's "Cass I got him" I hit him and ran then jumped into a cab and was gone before other units could respond fast enough I then told the cab driver to bring me to my house. Once I got to my house I called my mother as she cried on the other end of the phone "Jacob what's going on?" I just seen on television what they are saying about you all the horrible things please come home i've been calling you for days please son I love you so much I can't lose you too. I replied mom your not going to lose me i'm coming I will explain everything to you when I get there. She replied when are you coming? I replied I can't take a plane to risky I will get caught so I have to take a bus it will be about a day and a half look I love you mom and I will see you soon. She then asked well when are you leaving Jacob? I replied tonight or tomorrow morning but most likely tonight look mom I have to go ok I love you and will talk to you soon. She replied I love you more get home safe son. I replied I will. But their was one more thing that I needed to do before I left I needed to know if my own bestfriend really ratted me out to the police or not I hadn't spoken to him since but it was time to make that call so I did. I asked Blake hey don't take this the wrong way bro but hey did you set that up? Blake replied set up what? I replied that back door thing with the L.A.P.D.? Blake replied I sware to you Jacob I promise that I never would do that to you in a million years you should know that bro please don't that that. Your lika a brother to me we do everything together i've always been by your side I had no idea he was coming back forreal. I replied why didn't you tell me that you knew the bartender from The Room club? Blake replied Jacob you never asked me. Blake continued what are you going to do now? I replied go find out who set me up. I was wrong all along I suspected Kayshawn hell even you listen to me everyone is a suspect but my investigating is taking me back to Washington.

Blake replied "wow" you suspected me? What's in Washington? I replied yes I do and that is what I need to find out. Look Blake i'm just confused as shit right now you would be to if you where in my shoes. Blake replied I understand bro. I replied listen Blake do you know where I can get a gun from? Blake replied why do you need a gun for Jacob? What the fuck is going on bro? I replied I don't know yet can you get one? Blake replied I probably can yeah when would you need it by? I replied by tonight if not don't worry about it. Blake replied i'll see what I can do bro you leaving tonight? I replied yes it's not safe for me out here anymore. Blake replied ok i'll see what I can do bro i'll call you back. I replied no I will get back intouch with you bro. Blake replied ok sounds good. But I had already left the house and the phone in the middle of the living room floor with a note saying "give me a few days Armstrong" Just in case he was listening in because that is how I believe he found me at the Hollywood Hotel Armstrong had traced my phone but if he traced it i'm sure he tapped it as well. Nevertheless I let him know my moves to let him know i'm not bullshitting. So back off to Aberdeen Washington I was headed to home sweet home to find out just what the fuck was going on and who this girl was. When I got to Washington I took a cab over to my mothers house it must of been 10:00am in the morning and I knocked on my mothers front door. The look on her face when she opened the door was a Thank god your ok look as tears of joy began to run down her face she said to me welcome back home son. I gave her a big huge hug and told her how much i've missed her as I stepped inside. The place looked exactly how it looked when I had left home years ago she hadn't changed a thing in her place. After I got settled in my mother asked me Jacob what is going on please talk to me? Why are they saying you murdered some girl? I replied ok look mom after I won the Kayshawn case my roommate thought it would be a good idea to go out and celebrate so we did. Well I end up meeting this really gorgeous woman we where dancing, talking, having some drinks and just having a good time you know? Well anyways she then invites me back to her place and one thing leads to another and well during our time together she just died just like that out of nowhere. Now I had to make a choice to either call the police and risk being their main suspect or just get the hell out of there and well I panicked and left. I met her roommate or friend whatever and she knew that I went to this woman apaprtment with her. Well when she went to go see her friend the next day she found her dead and just like that the police think I killed her which I didn't. Now if this story isn't crazy enough this woman who I met in the club lied to me and told me that she was from Miami come to find out that she really is from right here what a coincedent right? Wrong she also had never been to that club before it was her first time as well as mine doesn't that all sound strange to you? My mom replied oh my god Jacob what are you going to do? I replied well my plan is to find out who set me up. My mother replied ok and how do you plan on doing that? Well I first suspected Kayshawn's people maybe a teammate, a family member, or a friend, I don't know. Then I thought maybe it was my own friend and roommate but through investigating it lead me right back home so my only lead is following this mystery girl she told me that she was a hair dresser so here is what I need to do. I need to find out how many hair dressing places are in Aberdeen. My mother replied and then what? I replied well then I go to every last one of them until I find out which one she worked at. My mother replied what does she have to do with who set you up? I don't get it Jacob? I replied well for starters her girlfriend told me that this woman had never been to that club beforee that it was her first time going there and guess what mom? My mother replied what? I replied it was also my first time going there that is the first coinsident like I told you before the second is she is from Aberdeen Washinton just like me and lied about it now doesn't that seem odd to you mom? something fishy is going on so right now this woman is my only lead to go on. My mother replied ok so after you find out where she works at what then? I replied I don't know I guess I go from there. She replied ok Jacob just be safe ok? I replied always mom. So I got to work now in my investigative work I found out that their our 26 hair dressers in Aberdeen and I needed to hit them all asking if their were an Elizabeth West working here about two or three weeks ago. This went on for about three days of "no the name doesn't ring a bell" I hit 20 hair dressers in just 3 days and I got nowhere. Being that I was the hometown hero in Aberdeen nobody looked at me as a murderer these were my people I grew up out here so everyone was polite and very helpful only that name just didn't ring any bells to nobody that I had asked. Aberdeen isn't that big so most of the people here know of eachother or seen eachother atleast once or twice before. I was the biggest name in Aberdeen other then Kurt Kobain so people were very eager to help but to no luck. The news stations reporting the incident didn't even have a picture of this Elizabeth West because according to the news nobody had come fourth as a reletive or family member she had no pictures of herself in her apartment and niether did her friend it was almost as like she didn't even exist all around town I couldn't catch a break. It wasn't until I hit the 23rd hair dresser on my list a place called Studio Day Spa Hair dressers. When I walked in and asked to speak to the manager she came up and said yes Mr. Cass how can I help you? I replied yes Hi I need to know if you ever had a woman working here by the name of Elizabeth West? The manager lady replied umm no doesn't ring a bell why do you ask? I replied think real hard Ma'm she would of been working here if so about two or three weeks ago maybe a month ago at best a really beautiful and exotic looking woman she probably told you that she was headed to Los Angeles or something like that? Then the manager lady looked like she just had saw a ghost or something like that and replied "oh my god" Elizabeth is the woman in L.A. they are saying you murdered? I replied yes do you know her? The manager lady replied sadly "oh my god" yes I remember her she was a beautiful girl she didn't work here very long though it always seemed as if she was searching for something you know? Like a better life something or someone she was very different, very quiet, very observant, but a very good hairdresser though oh my god that poor girl what happened to her? And why are you calling her Elizabeth West? Did she change her name when she got to L.A. or something like that? She was always about change I told you. I replied wait what is her last name? She told me that it was West? The manager lady replied No that is the rich girl who lives in the big mansion on the hill her last name is Banks that's that rich guys daughter. As I was in total disbelief I said to myself

Banks? Rich girl? I couldn't believe it Elizabeth Banks as in Theodore Banks daughter? What the fuck? What the fuck is going on? You mean to tell me that girl was Theodore Banks daughter the guy who killed my father? That fucking Cocksucker set me up? I'm going to kill him once and for all. What the fuck is going on man? The manager lady says Mr. Cass are you alright? You look like you just seen a ghost or something. I replied yes i'm ok look thank you for all your help ma'm. The manager lady replied your welcome you sure your ok? Can I get you a glass of water or something? I replied no i'm ok thank you and I left. I left and drove as fast as I could to my mothers house I was so fucking pissed and confused this motherfucker set me up but I needed to find out why? Once I got back to my mothers house I said mom it's Banks as i'm pacing back and fourth throughout the house. She replied Jacob calm down what's going on? I replied Banks set me up that girl from the club is Theodore Banks daughter. My mother replied "oh my god" Jacob please just call the police and let them handle it don't do anything crazy please what are you going to do next Jacob? I replied i'm going to pay Banks a visit at his home and find out why he set me up. Then my mother saw me reach into one of my fathers dressers and pull out his gun he always kept in the house for protection. My mother said oh my god Jacob please don't do this let's just call the police son. I replied mom listen I love you with all my heart ok you know that but this shit comes to an end tonight he has taken almost everything from me. He took my father, possibly my career, my credibility, everything that I worked for and now possibly my freedom i'm not about to lose you too I have to end this. As my mother pleaded with me "Jacob please don't" if you love me please don't. I gave her a kiss on the cheek and hugged her goodbye I told her listen mom i'm headed over to Banks place now if I don't see you again for any reason I promise you that nobody will ever hurt you again. Crying my mother replied Jacob I can't lose you to please don't go. I replied I have to go mom and I left. I jumped back into her car and speed all the way to Theodore Banks mansion pulled up to the gate and hit the buzzer. A few buzzes went by and Theodore answers it and says Mr. Cass i've been expecting you let yourself in i'm in my office come on up. He then opened the gate and I speed all the way through got out the car so fast cocked and fucking loaded opened up his front door and ran all the way up the staircase looked for his office doors and when I found them I kicked those fucking doors open so fast to be greeted by Theodore sitting at a brown wooden office desk with a gun in his left hand pointed right at me as mine pointed right back at him. Banks says Cass sit down you don't need this to get ugly do you want some brandy or vodka? Cool, calm, and collective he was. I replied fuck you banks you set me up you fucking piece of shit I should fucking kill you. Banks replied oh like you did my daughter huh? So that's what you do nowadays your a murderer? The great Jacob Cass attorney turned killer you have made quite the name for yourself Cass. As I cock my gun back yet again i replied fuck you your a murderer not me. Why the fuck did you set me up for? You planned all this didn't you? Banks replied laughing you damn right I did son and I enjoyed every last minute of it but it's not over yet I saved the best part for last. I replied what the fuck do you want from me? Was killing my father not enough for you? What the fuck did I ever do to you?

You killed my father you son of a bitch. Banks replied loudly that is a good motherfucking question do let me explain. I want to tell you alittle story Cass you think me killing your father was an accident? I killed your father on purpose he destroyed my fucking life that's why I set you up i've been planning this for years son your father was having an afair with my fucking wife how do you like that Cass? I replied no your lying. Banks continues I caught him leaving my house on several occasions her are the pictures check them out for yourself as he tosses them over to me. My wife never treated me the same after that she looked at me differently she broke my heart and it was all because of your father. Banks continued so one day I got really drunk and I got into a rage a rage that needed to be fed so I decided to follow your father around studying his habits where he goes, what he does, all that and one night I caught him leaving the bar and I just blacked out and pushed the gas and closed my eyes. When I hit him with my car I was so relieved atleast I thought I was I got away with it and life went on. But then my wife became suddenly pregnant and as you know we where not having any sex what so ever while your father was in the picture. Mind you my wife thought all those years that I was blind to what she had been doing with your father but I wasn't I just was to in love with her to leave her. So she has this beautiful little baby girl who she passes off to be mine and I play along with it and help raise this child so this rage I had wouldn't die or go away because deep down inside I always knew the truth. So as this child grew older and older and her mother and I split up this rage grew anger and angrier and I would use her as a pawn to set up the great Jacob Cass. As your fame and popularity grew so did my anger towards your father, you, and this beautiful inoccent girl. So I told her to get close to you to set you up you know that whole daddy bullshit like sweety I want you to get with a good succsessful man and what not. So she flew out to Los Angeles and followed your every move just as I taught her. The club was her perfect execution to get close to you because you never go out and it worked to a fucking T. Only thing that I didn't tell poor Elizabeth was that I was killing two birds with one stone. You see the cocaine I had given her was laced with rat poising I told her that bag only to use when she makes contact with you it was a tough decision to make but it had to be done. But I guess Elizabeth had a conscience and had mercy on you so she sniffed the bag you both were suppose to sniff but she did that bag and gave you the regular cocaine. I guess you made a good impression on her or something like that but her apartment was set up by yours truly who watched in the wings. The letters, the tie, everything and it all worked great so in the end your sister Elizabeth Banks aka Cass is dead your father is dead and that only leaves you so are you ready to joining them now that you know the truth? It's either that or a cell? It's your choice Cass? I replied you are one sick twisted motherfucker you know that Banks? That was my fucking sister? But guess what Theodore Banks? Banks replied laughing what Cass? I replied that was a very lovely and touching confession you just made I recorded and is going straight to the police. So my only question to you Banks is it dead or Jail it's your decision Banks? Banks replied your bluffing with a scared look on his face. I replied what is this then I showed him the tape recorder and said so I guess this is goodbye Banks where done here have a good one and I turned around to go walk away as he was stunned. As I was walking away all I heard was "see you in hell Cass" and I heard the gun go off I thought I had been shot. But Banks had taken his own life as I then left back to my mothers house and called the police my mother was crying she was so happy to see me walk back through that front door again. She asked me Jacob what happened? I replied mom its over. When the Aberdeen police arrived at Banks house they found him sitting in his office chair dead. The Aberdeen police had been investigating me in coroperation with the L.A.P.D. so when the cops came to arrest me at my mothers home after i'm the one who called it in I handed over the recording to the lead Detective. Everything would be dropped against me because I finally gave Detective Armstrong a call and told him that I have the Banks confession recorded and when I fly back to Los Angeles I will personally hand it over to him. Aberdeen Police just let me go and told my mother and I to saty safe so that next morning bright and early I flew back out to Los Angeles and went straight to the L.A.P.D. with the recording and played it all for Detective Armstrong. He was impressed and blown away and just like that I was a free man but he did mention that I would have to pay a fine for hitting an officer laughing. In Armstrongs office he asked me was their anything that he could do for me? I told him actually there is I replied. Armstrong replied ok shoot. I replied I want my credibility back after my name was basked in the papers. Armstrong replied and how can I do that Cass? I replied well let's talk to the press together outside right here right now. Detective Armstrong replied you got it Cass. It went something like this "Business tycoon and millionaire Theodore Banks has committed suicide after attempting to frame top Attorney Jacob Cass in the murder of his own daughter Elizabeth Banks" I Detective Armstrong would like to state that Mr. Cass is innocent of this crime and all charges have been dropped against him and he will continue to practice law in the great state of California at the law firm of Almonds and Almonds any questions? "Mr. Cass?" "Mr. Cass?" as many reporters asked the question what are you going to do next Attorney Cass? I replied well i am writing a book about the events that took place from Theodore Banks to Kayshawn James. One reporter replied and what will you call it? I replied I think I will call it "Main Suspect" The defense rest it's case no further questions i'm done.

THE END

THANK YOU'S

Well first off i'd like to thank God for without him none of this would be possible. I want to thank my Beautiful, amazing, loving, parents Louis and Anna Miranda Thank you for everything you both ever did for me I couldn't ask for better parents. I hope that you both our proud of me because you never got to see me shine but I believe you both knew that I would one day. I love and miss you both so very much may you both rest in peace. Thank you to my loving, Beautiful queen my wife Jessica you have stood by my side throughout it all you have been with me at my lowest some of my hardest times in life you had to deal with it and it wasn't fair to you but its truly because of you that I was able to smile again and get back on my feet. Thank you for showing me how a real woman treats her man I love you Jess you are my other half. Thank you to my brother Dashaune you have had my back throughout it all the ups, the downs, the highs, the lows, I can always count on you bro even though your personality at times drives me crazy but I love you because of you the family is complete again. Thank you to my children May'lon, Shawn, JaSir, Malakai, you may or may not all be my biological children but the time i spent raising you all made me a better person and I was proud to be your dad. I will always be here for you all can't wait until the day I can be with you all again. I stay away because it hurts to have to leave but you all will understand when you are older I love you all. Thank you to my aunt Barbara, George "The Duke" Rollins, Davitt, Davone, Christopher "Righteous" Dorsey,

Ernesto, Melissa, Takis, Eddie, Mitchell, Denise, Joey, Ed, Jr, Samual "Jersey" Devault, Jeremey, Jenny, Kim, Josh, Dj, Josie, Sherm, Brandy, Phillip, Neil, Christina, John, Terri, John "B. Swag" Beeman, Andre, OBG, Authorhouse, Cash Money Content, The New Port Richey Public Library, The Main street food mart, Facebook, Twitter, Instagram, Jeff, Tj, Maan, Birdman, Slim, 50cent, Scott, Ken, The entire Miranda family, The entire Almonds family, The Rios family, my wild ass step son Dominic, every and anybody who looks out for me and supports me and loves me I thank you all. If I forgot to mention anybody I truly am sorry I just know way to many people please don't be upset with me. I truly do love you all god bless.

– May'lon "Maze" Miranda

I SAID

A Poem by

May'lon "Maze" Miranda

I SAID i lost my smile,

I SAID i lost my happiness,

I SAID i lost my direction,

I SAID i lost my hope,

I SAID i lost my sight,

I SAID i lost my faith,

I SAID i was lost in the dark but you gave me light.

I SAID i was weak but you gave me strength and made me strong. Now between you and Jesus Christ I can do no wrong.

Because it was you that I was seeking all along.

Thank you Jesus

ALCOHOL

A Poem by

May'lon "Maze" Miranda

ALCOHOL was new

ALCOHOL was real

ALCOHOL you knew just how to make me feel

ALCOHOL made me steal

ALCOHOL made me lie

ALCOHOL made me cry

ALCOHOL made me wish i would die

ALCOHOL why?

ALCOHOL you take me away

ALCOHOL even for a day

ALCOHOL I wish I could stay

ALCOHOL you changed me

ALCOHOL I love you

ALCOHOL I hate you

ALCOHOL if you were a woman I would fucking date you.

ALCOHOL you made me

ALCOHOL you played me

ALCOHOL you pain me

ALCOHOL you tamed me

ALCOHOL you trained me

ALCOHOL made me fight

ALCOHOL made me see the light

ALCOHOL made me feel oh so bright

ALCOHOL had me up all night

ALCOHOL I need you to make me feel right

but ALCOHOL if I don't divorce you I could die of liver cancer and that ain't right.

SO peace ALCOHOL goodnight.

BORN 2 DO THIS

A Poem by

May'lon "Maze" Miranda

Premature baby gods gift

almost didn't make it

but little did I know that I was

BORN 2 DO THIS.

Shy and quiet kid growing up had 2 step my game up

but little did I know that I was BORN 2 DO THIS.

With the rock in my hand couldn't be touched didn't know enough but little did I know that I was BORN 2 DO THIS.

All throughout my childhood and all throughout my schooling good kid couldn't do enough but little did I know that I was BORN 2 DO THIS.

Adoption had me fucked up could careless didn't give a fuck but little did I know that I was BORN 2 TO DO THIS.

A drop out had 2 get my weight up not my hate up but little did I know that I was BORN 2 DO THIS.

Love was so blind love was so deep because of that I had to creep but little did I know that I was BORN 2 DO THIS.

Got caught up the kid was in it 2 deep or was the kid just asleep? But little did I know that I was BORN 2 DO THIS.

With the ratchet in my hand couldn't understand that I was BORN 2 DO THIS.

Finally reunited with the fam maybe this was all gods plan that I was BORN 2 DO THIS.

Then I was off of papers and never felt safer maybe because I was BORN 2 DO THIS.

Woman of my life I turned into my wife because I was BORN 2 DO THIS.

Kids gave me life and now I do right because I was BORN 2 DO THIS.

Now you can read about my life and if I inspire you that means I'm mad nice.

So I guess in the end I was BORN 2 DO THIS

If you enjoyed this book

check out www.maylonmiranda.com for more

titles by book author and motivational speaker

May'lon "Maze" Miranda

visit us on the web FaceBook at May'lon Miranda

Twitter @Maylon Miranda

Instagram at author.maylon.maze.miranda

AuthorHouse / MirandaPublishing

Printed in the United States
By Bookmasters